GW00858960

A Pie to Die For

A Bakery Detectives Cozy Mystery

By
Stacey Alabaster

Copyright © 2016 Fairfield Publishing

ALL RIGHTS RESERVED. Except for review quotes, this book may not be reproduced, in whole or in part, without the written consent of the author.

This story is a work of fiction. Any resemblance to actual people, places, or events is purely coincidental.

Table of Contents

Introduction 1

Chapter 1 2

Chapter 2 13

Chapter 3 21

Chapter 4 47

Chapter 5 63

Chapter 6 81

Chapter 7 97

Chapter 8...107

Chapter 9...119

Epilogue 132

Introduction

Thank you so much for buying my book. I am excited to share my stories with you and hope that you are just as thrilled to read them.

If you would like to know about all my new releases and have the opportunity to get free books, make sure you sign up for our Cozy Mystery Newsletter.

FairfieldPublishing.com/cozy-newsletter

Stacey Alabaster

Chapter 1

I let out a little squeal as I brushed the foul, winged creature aside. "Not today buddy, not today!" I watched it intently as it flew away, a tiny black dot disappearing into the fall sky, and was glad that I hadn't needed to swat the poor thing. I heaved a sigh of relief as I took the lids off my desserts and a sweet cloud of vanilla, chocolate, and coffee bean, all mixed together, hit my nostrils.

That was the danger of serving food outdoors: flies. I was hoping that I'd seen the last of them for the day. Normally, I had my cakes and pastries sequestered safely away in my bakery, Rachael's Boutique Cakes. But today, being outside was a necessary evil. It was the annual Belldale Street Fair and it was my last chance to show the town that my cakes were worth stopping for, my last chance to save my failing bakery and keep the bank from serving me an eviction notice.

My fingers trembled as I removed the last of the lids and rearranged the decorations on my stall. I'd chosen a pink and white theme for the day and I piled cupcakes and macaroons high on a cute little pink cake stand, trying not to drop them with my shaking hands.

Meanwhile, I watched the numerous employees of the Bakermatic food tent set up their factory made cakes with soldier-like intensity. My stomach dropped as I saw a sign go up with "Free Samples" written on it.

I glanced at my own price tags. How was I ever going to compete with free samples? Slowly, I reached over and, with a black marker, slashed my prices in half.

It was going to be a long day.

***

Midday. Three hours into the fair and I'd had a total of four customers. Meanwhile, the Bakermatic tent a hundred feet away was bursting at the seams with people trying to claim their free samples, which never seemed to run out.

Maybe I should just pack up and take the cakes back to the store.

I saw a figure out of the corner of my eye waddling towards the stall.

Oh no, not this woman, I thought. The lady, middle-aged with cat-eyed spectacles and a streak of pink in the front of her otherwise brown hair, only ever seemed to come into my bakery for the sole purpose of tutting and telling me that my cakes were twice the price of the cakes and pastries that Bakermatic sold.

"But that's because mine are twice as good." I would try to reason with her, only to be met with a sharp lift of her eyebrows.

"I use quality ingredients. And I pay my staff a proper wage." After I would tell her that, I'd lean back with my arms crossed over my chest. She could hardly argue with paying people—students, single mothers—a living wage, right? Wrong. She always tutted and stuck up her nose before informing me, loudly, that she was going to take her business to Bakermatic instead. "I can get a coffee AND a cupcake there for the price of just a cupcake here!"

And it seemed like half the town followed her. Every day, more and more customers chose their low prices over my painfully handcrafted selection of cookies, cupcakes, and pastries. Thus the ever growing pile of bills on my kitchen table. And I thought going into business for myself at age twenty-five was going to be glamorous.

Now she was here. I bristled as she approached with bull-like intensity, her eyes focused on my table, waiting for her to cast more disparaging comments. She pointed to a fresh baked pie on my table. "I'll have a slice of that."

My face stretched into a wide smile. "Really?"

Her coin purse paused in midair. "Are you trying to turn away a customer?"

"No, of course not! Just surprised that you would want a piece of my pie. What with Bakermatic giving away free samples down the road."

She screwed her face up. "Don't worry! I'll be sampling theirs as well!" She threw my pie a look of disdain. "It's for my food blog. I've got to try something from every stall. So don't go getting a big head, thinking that I'd choose you over them!"

Of course not. "Your blog?" I watched eagerly as she sampled my pie. "Well, surely you'll have to give my pie a better review than Bakermatic's, despite the price. Mine are fresh, made from all local ingredients, all hand-made every day."

She cut me off and slammed the plate down on the table before scribbling something in her notebook. "I will be taking cost into account as well, don't you worry about that, young lady. I still don't know how you can get away with charging an arm and a leg for this!"

She picked up her piece of pie with disdain and walked away—heading straight for the Bakermatic stand. I stood there with my mouth hanging open before I remembered I was supposed to be attracting customers, not repelling them. I tightened my apron and put on my brightest smile as a man with ginger hair and a portly waist line hurried past.

"Hey!" I said, throwing him my best flirtatious smile as I tried to usher him back to my stand. "You gotta try one of these."

He screwed his nose up. "I think I'll try one from Bakermatic instead." He patted his oversized tummy before adding, "Gotta watch the calories, you know. I can't have too many."

"But mine are made from all natural ingredients." Ahhh, it was too late. He was already waddling towards the Bakermatic stand, like they needed one more customer to add to the overflowing mob already crowding their tent.

I sighed. What was the use? How could I compete with thousands of free samples? This street fair was supposed to be my way to attract more customers, to get the word out that I had the best baked goods in town, and I couldn't even get anyone to stop and try them.

"Hey there," a kind voice called out. "Why are you looking so sad for?"

I glanced up. There he was. Tall, dark floppy hair. I guessed he was about five years older than me, which was just about perfect. Five years older and five inches taller.

A grin swept over my face in spite of myself. "Nothing," I said hurriedly, scurrying to tidy all the rows of unsold cakes and pies. Must look professional. Must look successful.

"Aww come on," he said, with a smile that brightened the damp day. "A gorgeous girl like you, with cakes that look so good. What's got you down so bad?"

I sighed. "That's very kind of you to say. But even though my cakes might look good," I brushed over his compliment about my own appearance. "it doesn't mean they're selling." I pointed down the road to the line that snaked out of the Bakermatic tent. "I think they've got the monopoly on baked goods."

"Ah, I've heard about them." He nodded slowly and pursed his lips. "They're supposed to be evil, right?"

"Pure evil." I raised my eyebrows and let out a little

laugh.

"Well, I'd rather try one of yours."

He cast me a lingering look that made the butterflies in my stomach take flight. I perused the table, trying to find the best piece for him. I settled on my delicate carrot cake with cream cheese frosting and little red heart-shaped dots sprinkled on top. *Too much?* I told myself I'd explain that I hadn't noticed the hearts if he pointed them out.

He took the cake and—was it my imagination?—smiled a little when he saw the heart-shaped sprinkles. "Very nice," he said before opening his mouth wide.

It was a nervous few seconds before he gave his verdict.

"Perfect." He dusted off his hands and nodded. "If all your cakes are this good, I think I'll be seeing you again very soon. Rachael, wasn't it?" He nodded at the shop sign name.

"That's me." I grinned. "And you are?"

"Jackson. I'll be seeing you again soon, Rachael."

As I watched him walk away, I grinned to myself, my stomach warm and gooey as a cupcake fresh from the oven. Maybe today wasn't such a disaster after all.

***

I kicked off my heels. As soon as I sat down there was a knock on the door. Great timing.

But I grinned when I saw Pippa's shock of red curls peaking through the windows. After the day I'd had, I'd forgotten what day it was. Time for Criminal Point.

Pippa had her hair tucked under a baseball cap wearing the logo of a company I didn't recognize. She threw it off and it rolled under one of my designer chairs. "How did it go today?"

I held my hands up. "I don't even want to talk about it." Not even the cute stranger, although that was the kind of thing I usually shared with Pippa. But talking about Mr. Handsome was going to mean dredging up all the other junk: the unsold cakes, the bills piling up at the door, the imminent eviction notice. I slumped back onto the sofa.

"All I want to do is lie here, tune out, and watch some TV."

"What's on the box tonight?"

I grinned at her. "Pippa, you know very well what

night it is."

She stuck her tongue out. "Shall I order the pizza?"

I nodded gratefully. "Pepperoni thin crust! You know the deal. We always order the same thing."

***

Five minutes of Criminal Point left to go. The on screen detectives had just reached that point where the light bulb goes off and they were about to burst through the door of the final suspect, the one who had committed the murder.

Pippa and I leaned over, breaths held, pizza cheese dripping onto our plate below. Just as they were about to reveal the killer, the broadcast was interrupted for an "Important Local News Update."

"Nooo!" I squealed, reaching for the remote, stabbing at it randomly as though I could bring the program back to life. "What happened!"

"Shh," Pippa said. I felt her nails dig into my bicep. "Listen!" Pippa hissed for me to be quiet.

"What?"

"Shh!"

I dropped my pizza as a shot of the street fair flashed onto the screen. My mouth dropped as the anchor, a woman with a helmet of blonde hair and a stern face, delivered the news. "A woman has died following the Belldale Annual Street Fair, and police suspect that foul play may have been at work. They are investigating suspects now, and are urging anyone with details to come forward." An image of the victim flashed onto the box. Middle-aged, brown hair with a pink streak down the front. Her name was Colleen Batters.

Pippa and I stared to look at each other. "I know that woman!"

Pippa gulped. "How? Rachael, please tell me you just know her from your book club or something?"

I shook my head. "I served her today. Oh, Pippa! She was one of the few people to actually eat at my stand!" My heart started thumping and my head felt like it was pumped full of helium. Had I killed Colleen? My mind started fumbling back through the day's events, to all the other people who'd eaten my food. What about that cute guy? Jackson. Was he okay?

There was a knock on the door. I was too stunned to even stand up so Pippa bounced over and pulled it open.

A voice on the other side cleared his throat. "I'm looking for a Miss Robison."

Pippa turned slowly to look at me. "It's a cop," she mouthed in an exaggerated way with her eyes popped.

I walked over to the door like a zombie.

There he was. "Jackson?"

He cleared his throat again. "Officer Whitaker actually, under these circumstances. Miss Robinson, I'm afraid I need you to come in and answer a few questions. You're under suspicion for the murder of Mrs. Colleen Batters."

Chapter 2

"But you don't understand, I use only the finest, organic ingredients." My voice was high-pitched as I pleaded my case to the policeman. Oh, this was just like an episode of Criminal Point. Hey, I wondered who the killer turned out to be. I shook my head. That's not important, Rachael, I scolded myself. *What's important is getting yourself off this murder charge.* Still, I hoped Pippa had recorded the ending of the episode.

I tried to steady my breathing as Jackson—Detective Whitaker—entered the room and threw a folder on the table, before studying the contents as though he was cramming for a test he had to take the next day. He rubbed his temples and frowned.

Is he even going to make eye contact with me? Is he just going to completely ignore the interaction we had at the fair? Pretend it never even happened.

"Jackson..." I started, before I was met with a steely glare. "Detective. Surely you can't think I had anything to do with this?"

Jackson looked up at me slowly. "Had you ever had

any contact with Mrs. Batters before today?"

I shifted in my seat. "Yes," I had to admit. "I knew her a little from the store. She was always quite antagonistic towards me, but I'd never try to kill her!"

"Witnesses near the scene said that you two had an argument." He gave me that same steely glare. Where was the charming, flirty, sweet guy I'd meet earlier? He was now buried beneath a suit and a huge attitude.

"Well...it wasn't an argument...she was just...winding me up, like she always does."

Jackson shot me a sharp look. "So, she was annoying you? Was she making you angry?"

"Well... Well..." I tripped over my words. He was now making me nervous for an entirely different reason than he had earlier. Those butterflies were back, but now they felt like daggers.

Come on, Rach. Everyone knows that the first suspect in Criminal Point is not the one that actually did it.

But how many people had Jackson already interviewed? Maybe he was saving me for last. Gosh, maybe my cherry pie had actually killed the woman!

"Answer the question please, Miss Robinson."

"Not angry, no. I was just frustrated."

"Frustrated?" A smile curled at his lips before he pounced. "Frustrated with Mrs. Batters?"

"No! The situation. Come on—you were there!" I tried to appeal to his sympathies, but he remained a brick wall.

"It doesn't matter whether I was there or not. That is entirely besides the point." He said the words a little too forcefully.

I swallowed. "I couldn't get any customers to try my cakes, and Bakermatic was luring everyone away with their free samples." I stopped as my brows shot up involuntarily. "Jackson! Sorry, Detective. Mrs. Batters ate at Bakermatic as well!"

My words came out in a stream of breathless blabber as I raced to get them out. "Bakermatic must be to blame! They cut corners, they use cheap ingredients. Oh, and I know how much Mrs. Batters loved their food! She was always eating there. Believe me, she made that very clear to me."

Jackson sat back and folded his arms across his chest. "Don't try to solve this case for us."

I sealed my lips. *Looks like I might have to at this rate.*

"We are investigating every place Mrs. Batters ate today. You don't need to worry about that."

I leaned forward and banged my palm on the table. "But I do need to worry about it! This is my job, my livelihood...my life on the line. If people think I am to blame, that will be the final nail in my bakery's coffin!" Oh, what a day. And I'd thought it was bad enough that I hadn't gotten any customers at my stand. Now I was being accused of killing a woman!

I could have sworn I saw a flicker of sympathy finally crawl across Jackson's face. He stood up and readjusted his tie, but he still refused to make full eye contact. "You're free to go, Miss Robinson," he said gently. There was that tone from earlier, finally. He seemed recognizable as a human at long last.

"Really?"

He nodded. "For the moment. But we might have some more questions for you later, so don't leave town."

I tried to make eye contact with him as I left, squirreling out from underneath his arm as he held the door open for me, but he just kept staring at the floor.

Did that mean he wasn't coming back to my bakery after all?

Pippa was still waiting for me when I returned home later that evening. There was a chill in the air, which meant that I headed straight for a blanket and the fireplace when I finally crawled in through the door. Pippa shot me a sympathetic look as I curled up and crumbled in front of the flames. *How had today gone so wrong, so quickly?*

"I recorded the last part of the show," Pippa said softly. "If you're up for watching it."

I groaned and lay on the carpet, my back straight against the floor like I was a little kid. "I don't think I can stomach it after what I just went through. Can you believe it? Accusing ME of killing Mrs. Batters? When I *know* that Bakermatic is to blame. I mean, Pippa, they must be! But this detective wouldn't even listen to me when I was trying to explain Bakermatic's dodgy practices to him."

Pippa leaned forward and took the lid off a pot, the smell of the brew hitting my nose. "Pippa, what is that?"

She grinned and stirred it, which only made the

smell worse. I leaned back and covered my nose. "Thought it might be a bit heavy for you. I basically took every herb, tea, and spice that you had in your cabinet and came up with this! I call it 'Pippa's Delight'!"

"Yeah well, it doesn't sound too delightful." I sat up and scrunched up my nose. "Oh, what the heck—pour me a cup."

"Are you sure?" Pippa asked with a cheeky grin.

"Go on. I'll be brave."

I braced myself as the brown liquid hit the white mug.

It was as disgusting as I had imagined, but at least it made me laugh when the pungent concoction hit my tongue. Pippa always had a way of cheering me up. If it wasn't her unusual concoctions, or her ever changing hair color—red this week but pink the last, and purple a week before that—then it was her never-ending array of careers and job changes that entertained me and kept me on my toes. When you're trying to run your own business, forced to be responsible day in and day out, you have to live vicariously through some of your more free-spirited friends. And Pippa was definitely that: free-spirited.

"Hey!" I said suddenly, as an idea began to brew in

my brain. I didn't know if it was the tea that suddenly brought all my senses to life or what it was, but I found myself slamming my mug on the table with new found enthusiasm. "Pippa, have you got a job at the moment?" I could never keep up with Pippa's present state of employment.

She shrugged as she kicked her feet up and lay back on the sofa. "Not really! I mean, I've got a couple of things in the works. Why's that?"

I pondered for a moment. "Pippa, if you could get a job at Bakermatic, you could see first hand what they're up to!" My voice was a rush of excitement as I clapped my hands together. "You would get to find out the ways they cut corners, the bad ingredients they use, and, if you were really lucky, you might even overhear someone say something about Mrs. Batters!"

A gleam appeared in Pippa's green eyes. "Well, I do need a job, especially after today."

I raced on. "Yes! And you've got plenty of experience working in cafes."

"Yeah. I've worked in hundreds of places." She took a sip of the tea and managed to swallow it. She actually seemed to enjoy it.

"I know you've got a lot of experience. You're sure to

get the job. They're always looking for part-timers."
Unfortunately, Bakermatic was planning on expanding
the storefront even further, and that meant they were
looking for even more employees to fill their big yellow
store. "Pippa, this is the perfect plan! We'll get you an
application first thing in the morning. Then you can
start investigating!"

Pippa raised her eyebrows. "Investigating?"

I nodded and lay my head back down on the carpet.
"Criminal Point—Belldale Style! Bakery Investigation
Unit! I will investigate and do what I can from my end as
well! Perhaps I could talk to people from all the other
food stalls! Oh, Pippa, we're going to make a crack team
of detectives!"

"The Bakery Detectives!"

We both started giggling but, as the full weight of the
day's events started to pile up on me, I felt my stomach
tighten. It might seem fun to send Pippa in to spy on
Bakermatic, but this was serious. My bakery, my
livelihood, and even my own freedom depended on it.

Chapter 3

"You look amazing, don't worry," I said, covering my mouth to hide my laughter as I tried to swallow it.

Pippa looked herself up and down in the full-length mirror in my hallway. "This is the ugliest uniform I've ever been made to wear, and believe me, I've worn a few."

On any other day, I would have been the first to admit that the scratchy yellow polyester shirts Bakermatic forced their employees to wear was the worst thing my eyes had ever seen (except for their week old, pre-packaged cakes), but I was trying to convince Pippa that her new job was a good idea, and I couldn't let this yellow monstrosity get in the way.

"It's fine." I assured her, though I could still feel the tears prickling my eyes. "It goes with your hair."

Pippa turned, hands on her hips. "Bright red hair with bright yellow? I look like a clown."

I spun her back around. "It's only for a few days Pippa, maybe a week. Two weeks at the most."

She sighed and attached the neon yellow visor to her

head. "I still don't know if this is a good idea, Rach. What if I can't find anything? What if I get caught snooping around? You know how ruthless the Bakermatic Company is. What if they find out I'm there to spy on them?"

"Well, don't let them find out."

Pippa turned back and gave me a reluctant smile. "I want to do this for you, Rach, I really do."

"So then, what's the problem?" Cripes, I could tell that Pippa was losing her nerve. And she had a pretty strong nerve. Was she really that scared of Bakermatic's lawyers?

"You know me, Rach!" She sighed heavily and her shoulders slumped. "I'm always screwing everything up. I'll probably put salt in someone's coffee on my very first shift and get fired right away. Then I'll be no good to you at all! I'm going to let you down, Rach."

"Hey." I put my hands on Pippa's shoulders. "You're not going to let me down. I have faith in you, Pips. All you gotta do is go in there, keep your head down, try not to put any salt in anyone's coffee, and we'll be good." I felt my stomach clench. It all sounded simple enough, but I knew Pippa, and nothing was ever simple with her. Still, I tried to keep my face positive.

Pippa nodded. "You're forgetting one very important thing, though."

"Am I?"

"Find out what Bakermatic did to Colleen, and find the evidence to put them away."

I nodded. "Right," I said with determination. "We're going to prove that they poisoned Colleen Batters, and maybe—just maybe—my little bakery will survive."

***

10 AM. The perfect time to relax; take a little time and have some coffee and a cupcake.

At least, so you would think. The customers—or rather, the lack of them—at my store told a different story.

I sighed and sat down on my stool, untying my apron and throwing it on the bench. There was only so many times I could rearrange the cake stands and wipe the benches before I went out of my mind. I glanced around. The bakery was so clean it glistened, the baby pink and white surfaces so clean you could eat off them. And behind the glass cases, there was row after row of designer donuts, exotically flavored macaroons, gourmet cakes, and homemade pies. A sign advertising the ten o'clock coffee and cake special was flying in vain.

There wasn't a single customer in the shop.

I shook my head and muttered to myself for a second. "I bet that cop, Detective Whitaker, leaked the details of the case. Does everyone know I was taken in for questioning?"

Clearly. My reputation had been dashed.

I leaned forward and tried to peer down the street. I snapped back once my fears were confirmed. There was a line out of Bakermatic ten feet long. They'd clearly mopped up all my ten o'clock customers.

I sprung out of my seat when I heard the bell above the door jingle. "Hello there! Oh." My face dropped when I saw that it was just the mailman. He had a stack of little white envelopes for me, and I felt that clenching in my stomach again.

The mailman scrunched up his bald head and surveyed my empty store. "I wasn't sure you were even open by the looks of it from the outside."

"Well, we are open," I said, trying to remain bright as I ripped the top envelope open. "I couldn't interest you in one of my homemade selections, could I? How about..." I stopped and sized him up, coming up with just the perfect desert for him. "A slice of cherry pie?"

For just a moment, a look of temptation crossed his face and I could tell he was considering it. But then his face fell and he looked at the tiled floors before muttering an awkward, "Uh, no... I, uh, better not."

He hurried to the door.

"Hey, wait!" I called out after him.

He stopped, the door half pulled open. The bell above gave a sick little cough of a jingle. His back tensed and I knew he just wanted to escape before I asked him any more questions, or tried to force any more of my baked goods down his throat.

He turned back slowly and I read the name tag on his grey shirt. Gavin.

"Gavin," I said, still trying to remain upbeat and nonchalant, as though I was just innocently wondering the following question. "Is there any particular reason you don't want to try my cherry pie?"

He fidgeted for a second as he pretended to look at the price list. "It's just a little too expensive for me, miss."

Like I hadn't heard that one a hundred times before. I plastered on my brightest smile. "Oh, don't worry about the price," I said, swooping my arm around my mouth-watering selection of glossy pastries. "For you, Gavin, today, a slice is on the house. As a reward for all your hard work." And all the bills you delivered to me.

His mouth dropped open slightly and he handled the doorknob with an increasingly slippery palm. He patted his stomach. "That's generous of you, miss, but I'm real full right now. I had a big breakfast: eggs, sausages, and two pieces of toast."

I folded my arms. "You can take it with you and eat it later."

"Well, er, if I can eat it later," Gavin said, a look of relief flooding his face. "Then that should be fine."

"You can eat it later, as long as you have one little bite now," I cut him off. "Will that also be fine?"

I could see the beads of sweat forming on his brow. "Oh...ah...erm..."

I let out a short exhale. "I thought as much. Gavin, just tell me. Just give it to me straight. Why won't you eat any of my baked goods?"

He swallowed and I could see all the veins in his

neck pop out like they were trying to escape through his skin. "No...no reason, miss. I already told you, I'm real stuffed full right now..."

"Come on, Gavin. Cut it out."

He let the door fall shut. "Well, it's just... I'm afraid if I eat one of your cakes..." He glanced around the tins and cabinets. "Or pies, or pastries, or donuts. Well, I'm afraid..."

"You're afraid you might die?" I asked boldly, looking him straight in the eye.

He sighed. "I didn't want to say anything, miss. Didn't want to hurt your feelings. I see how hard you try in this store, and I got a daughter about your age, you kinda remind me of her. So I don't like to make things harder on you than they already are."

I felt bad all of a sudden that I hadn't even known Gavin's name 'til a few minutes earlier. I'd just always thought of him as "that man who brings me my bills" or, today, "that man who is trying to escape my clutches without telling me the truth."

"I didn't know you had a daughter, Gavin. What does she do?"

His face softened. "She's just finishing her medical

degree. I'm real proud of her. She'll be starting her first year residency soon."

I sighed internally. Being a doctor sounded a lot better than being a baker right now. "My father always wanted me to study medicine," I said wistfully. "Perhaps I should have taken his advice."

I slumped against the counter.

"Hey there," Gavin said, taking a step towards me, though still eyeing the cakes as though they were venomous creatures that might leap out and bite him. "Don't look so sad. I'm sure things will turn around."

I raised my eyebrows. "You're too scared to even take a bite of my pie. Gavin, what are people saying about me?"

He scratched the back of his neck. "Aw, it ain't so bad."

"Please. Tell me."

He looked at the floor and shrugged. "You know how people gossip. There are rumors flying around that you got taken in to the station, that they think your pie killed Colleen Batters."

"But everyone who took part in the street fair got taken in for questioning! The cops only talked to me as a precaution. To rule me out. They said anyone could be to blame." I pointed down the road at the overflowing line out the front of Bakermatic. "Even Bakermatic got brought in for questioning. Yet people aren't scared to eat there."

Gavin shook his head. "That's not what I heard, miss."

I spun around to look at him. "What do you mean?"

He shook his head. "I ain't heard that Bakermatic got brought in for questioning. In fact, their employees are telling every one that the only suspect is you. That you've been told not to leave town, and that it's only a matter of time before you're arrested for the murder of Colleen Batters."

My jaw dropped to the floor. Well, that explained the wasteland that my bakery had become. As if Bakermatic didn't have any problems soaking up my customer base on the best of days, undercutting my prices and stealing my ideas, now they were telling people my cake had killed Colleen?

"Thank you for being honest with me, Gavin," I said, ushering him out the door. "If you don't mind, I have some business to attend to."

He tried to protest for a moment. "It doesn't look

like you've got much business to attend to," he said, clutching his mailbag to his chest.

"Thanks for pointing that out." I waited until he was out the door before I turned the sign over to closed. "But it's not bakery business I've got to attend to."

It was detective business. I dusted my hands off and locked the door as Gavin tried to peer in through the windows, confusion clouding his face. If Bakermatic was going to try and pin the blame on me, then I was going to have to dedicate all my time to proving they were really the ones who killed Colleen Batters. I leaned against the cold glass door. *The nerve of them. They steal all my customers, and now they try and pin a murder charge on me!*

I pulled out my phone. Time to text Pippa.

***

It seemed like it took forever for Pippa to get back to me. *Don't tell me she's actually being responsible and not taking her phone out at work for once.*

Finally, just after 11:30, she texted me back. I grabbed my phone and glanced out the window while I read it.

Sorry Rach, so busy! First there was training and then we got slammed with a bunch of new customers. Wonder where they all came from?

My hands sped across my phone screen in a blur.

They came from my store Pips! There are practically tumbleweeds blowing through here. Have you heard anything yet? Is anyone talking about me or my store?

It took ages for her reply to come through, and as I waited, a sinking feeling entered my gut, like when I was trying to ferret the information from Gavin. Her silence spoke volumes.

Finally her reply came back.

Not much. Just a few rumors.

I stuck my phone back in my apron pocket. She didn't have to elaborate. Gavin was right, then. Bakermatic was telling everyone that I'd killed Colleen. I wondered if Pippa was even out there defending my honor.

Well, it was time to stop standing around waiting. I had Pippa in there as my eyes and ears, but I needed to do more. I needed to take advantage of her new position.

I pulled my phone back out. **Pippa I need you to sneak me into the store. I need to look in their kitchen. Maybe go through their paperwork.**

What? I can't do that! I could lose my job.

I held back from telling her that was only a matter of time, regardless of whether she did this for me or not.

We'll be careful. I need to see the place for myself Pips. Please. The store is dying. I need to do something.

OK. Once my shift is finished. I'm closing the store with another girl. I'll make up an excuse for why I need to hang back. I'll see you here after six. Don't come until it's dark.

Got it Pips. See ya at six.

***

Belldale looked particularly pretty as the light began to disappear from the sky and the stars started to make their first appearance. I shivered in my red peacoat as a sudden bolt of hope radiated through me. *Maybe it's going to be all right. Maybe I can sneak in, find some evidence, clear my name, and my bakery will thrive while Bakermatic goes under.*

"Psst!" I heard Pippa call. I squinted, trying to make her out in the dim light. She gestured for me to join her.

"A bright red coat, Rach? Really?"

I pouted a little. She was right, though. All the detectives on Criminal Point wore black or navy overcoats. You didn't see them gallivanting about, solving crimes in bright red. Still, it was dark so I didn't think it would matter too much.

"Stay here. We have to wait for Simona to clear out." Simona was Pippa's shift manager. Pippa had been telling me via text message that Simona was distracted due to a breakup with her boyfriend. Perfect, I'd thought. She might just let her guard down.

"What are you going to tell her?" I whispered. It was only Pippa's first day at Bakermatic, and it was going to take a lot of trust from the company to allow her to lock up on her own on her first day, even with a heartbroken shift manager in charge.

"I'm gonna wait till we're both done. Then, just as we're leaving, I'm gonna tell her I left my jacket inside, and ask to borrow the key." Pippa winked at me. "I've been buttering her up all day, being really sympathetic about the breakup with her boyfriend Charles, who seems like a real jerk, by the way."

Pippa suddenly pushed me out of the way and commanded me to be quiet. Behind her, a sniffling woman in her mid-twenties with a long dark ponytail walked out. "He hasn't returned any of my messages all day!" she wailed, shoving her phone in Pippa's face.

I pushed my back up against the wall and tried to remain flat, feeling the rough edges of the brick through my peacoat, which had been designed for fashion and not for practicality.

Pippa murmured her sympathy as she stared at the message-less screen. "Simona, honestly, you're too good for him. You're so pretty, and smart, and a manager already at your young age!" Pippa shot me a covert wink as she grabbed Simona by the shoulders so that she was facing away from me. "You don't need him, girl."

Simona sniffled and laughed a little. "You're right. You're so sweet, Pippa. I'm so glad you came to work here!"

I smiled to myself in the dark. It looked like Pippa had done a good job of worming her way in. Simona turned the key in the lock and they both walked towards the parking lot opposite me, until I saw Pippa stop suddenly and begin her charade. "I'll give the key back to you in the morning, Simona," she said, voice dripping with sweetness as she patted the other woman on the back. "You don't need to wait for me."

"I'm not sure, Pippa."

"Come on, Simona, it looks like you really need some rest."

"Eek!" Simona let out a squeal and jumped up and down excitedly. "He just texted me! He texted me!" Her eyes ran across the screen hungrily. "Oh, Pippa, if you don't mind just letting yourself back in, I really need to go. He wants to see me!"

Pippa's mouth spread into a wide grin, which was matched only by my own. "No, that's fine. You go!"

Pippa hurried back to me as Simona ran in the opposite direction.

She jangled the keys in front of me with a wild grin. "That worked out even better than I'd planned."

"You're a genius Pips. You always seem to shmooze up to the right people, no matter what job you get."

"It's a gift." She let out a short sigh. "Just too bad that I don't have a gift for actually keeping jobs."

I shot her a sympathetic look as she pushed the door open, and finally, we were inside, and alone.

"So this is what an evil lair looks like." I spun around the pristine looking kitchen with its stainless steel pantries and countertops. "It's a little disappointing."

Pippa flicked another light on. "I'm still not sure what you're hoping to find in here, Rach."

I shot her a look. "Anything." I hurried past her.

"Where's the office?"

Pippa was hot on my heels. "It's 'round the corner, to the right, but it's for managers only."

I spun around. "So what?"

Pippa stopped. "Well, it's locked."

I glanced down at the keys in Pippa's hand. "Isn't Simona a manager?"

She slowly lifted up the jangling bunch of keys. "She's only a shift manager. I'm not sure these will work."

I grabbed her by the arm. "Come on, we have to try."

"Okay, but quickly." Pippa looked over her shoulder. "Who knows how long we've got before someone calls security. You've already been to the police station once in the past twenty-four hours, you don't really want to make a second trip, do you?"

I kept a lookout while Pippa tried every key on the key chain with no luck. "Last one," she said, raising an eyebrow as she showed me our last hope of breaking into the office. "Wish me luck."

I took my eyes away from the hallway while I watched the key inch its way into the lock, and finally, after an eternity of waiting, click as it slotted in just the right way and allowed the door handle to turn.

"Phew," I said. "Thought we were going to have to break in for a second there."

Pippa raised an eyebrow. "Isn't that what we're already doing?"

"No, this is still legitimate," I rationalized. "You forgot your jacket, and we're just looking for it. You think it might be in this office." When Pippa still didn't look convinced, I added, "Breaking in—real breaking in—would have been if you'd had to pick the lock."

"Hey," Pippa said in mock offense. "What makes you assume I know how to pick locks?"

I gave her a look. "You don't?"

"Well, I do, but that's not the point!"

I laughed as I gently pushed her into the room. "Come on, let's go!"

I began to sift through the piles of papers on the desk. It was mostly mundane stuff—staff rosters, lists of stock to order for the following day, health and safety memos—while Pippa kept an eye out at the door. "Rachael, what are you looking for exactly? Do you really think there's going to be a piece of paper with 'We Killed Colleen Batters' written on it in bold text?"

"No, of course not." I continued to shuffle through the piles, not caring too much if I messed them up. "I'm just looking for something that shows how dodgy Bakermatic is, something that I can take to the police and show them."

"Rachael, careful! They're going to know someone was in here if you keep flinging the papers around like that! And they'll know I was in here because I had the key!"

"Oh, you're right," I said, hurrying to pick up the papers I'd knocked on the floor. It wasn't going to help my case if Pippa lost her job on day one.

"Here, let me help." Pippa raced over and knelt down on the floor, helping me put the stacks back in order. She frowned. "Does this look right? Is this what they looked like when we walked in?"

"I'm not--" I stopped speaking and brought my finger up to my lips.

"What is it?" Pippa whispered.

"Shh." I kept my finger pressed against my lips. Just as I was about to relax a little, I heard them again: footsteps.

"Oh cripes, someone's called security!" Pippa tried to

crawl under the desk. "We need to hide!"

I frantically looked around the room. There was only one cabinet along with the desk, and any attempt to spring out the door would only take us straight to the owner of those footsteps, which were drawing closer and closer. Pippa was right, the best option was under the desk. But was there enough room for the both of us?

Pippa pulled me in after her, not allowing me to make the decision or second-guess myself.

I heard her swearing under her breath as the steps drew closer. A pair of small feet in black boots appeared in the crack underneath the desk.

"Pippa?" a voice called out.

Not security after all. It was Simona. Pippa could barely conceal the groan that escaped and I shut my eyes, hoping that Simona hadn't heard it.

"Pippa," Simona said in a stern, booming voice. "Where are you? If you've broken into this office..."

So maybe Pippa had been right. Maybe it was technically breaking in. I felt her nails dig into my forearm again and I could hear her mutter, "Oh no, not again."

The footsteps drew closer and I sucked in my breath

and held it tight as a long brown ponytail appeared in front of the desk, swinging in front of us. Within seconds, Simona was down on her knees, her eyes glowing as she captured her prey.

"Simona, I can explain." Pippa said, clambering out of the desk. "I was... I was just looking for my jacket."

"Underneath the desk?" Simona already had her phone out and I could see her fingers taping 911.

Oh no!

"Please," I said, scrambling out after Pippa. "You don't need to call the cops. I can explain what we're doing here."

Simona's finger froze above the phone and her jaw dropped open. "Are you the girl from the bakery down the road? The one who has been killing people?"

"Yes...I mean, no! Not killing people!"

Her fingers jabbed frantically at the screen. "Police, please! We've had a break in at the Belldale Bakermatic Company, and the suspects are extremely dangerous."

I rolled my eyes while beside me, I noticed Pippa drop her head to the floor, all her usual enthusiasm drained from her. "Simona, does this mean?"

"Yes, Pippa. You are definitely fired."

***

Pippa was still grumbling when we finally got to the station. "She doesn't even have the power to fire me. She's only the shift manager, for crying out loud." The heat was off in the station and I shivered inside my red peacoat. It really was not built for sleuthing, or getting caught sleuthing. I made a mental note to buy a more practical coat in the future if we were going to keep up this detective work.

"Pippa, that isn't the most important issue right now," I started to say, before a tall man wearing an expensive navy suit strolled in with an arrogant swagger.

I groaned inwardly. *Nooo, not him.* This was exactly the last thing I had wanted to happen.

He shot me a sly grin. "Fancy seeing you in here again, Miss Robinson. Will you follow me please?"

"Good luck," Pippa whispered, shivering besides me. "He looks terrifying."

I braced myself for Jackson—Detective Whitaker— to give me another dressing down. I knew what he was going to say.

This doesn't look good for you, Rachael. Caught breaking and entering while you are suspected of killing a woman.

He was going to turn the screws, try to get me to confess while I was under stress. Not that I had anything to confess. But he didn't know that. I knew how guilty I looked.

Jackson kicked back in his seat and a wry smiled danced on his lips as he dangled a pen from them. "Not exactly keeping yourself inconspicuous, are you?"

Was this casual, friendly banter a way to unnerve me, a tactic to make me feel as though I could confide in him, open up?

"No," I had to admit. "I didn't exactly intend on ending up in the police station two nights in a row."

"What were you doing in the Bakermatic premises, Rachael?"

So, it was 'Rachael' now, rather than 'Miss Robinson.'

I decided to go with the truth. "I was trying to find evidence."

"Evidence of what?"

"Evidence that they did it. That they killed Colleen."

The wry grin was still on his lips but an edge of surprise had crept into his expression. "What did I tell you about not doing my job for me, Rachael?"

"I know. But you wouldn't listen to me last night when I tried to tell you that Bakermatic must be to blame."

"Rachael, you sound kind of obsessed with Bakermatic."

I leaned back in my seat. "I'm not obsessed with them. I just can't stand them. They've put me out of business, Jackson." I didn't stop and correct myself by calling him Detective. "And now they're telling people that I killed Colleen. My bakery was dead today. I didn't make a single sale."

"Well, I'm sorry to hear that." He sounded genuine. "But that doesn't give you the right to break into private property."

"But we had a key," I tried to protest.

"You're being charged with breaking and entering," Jackson said matter-of-factly as he scribbled something across a piece of paper. "And I'm sorry to say, this doesn't look good for you regarding the other matter,

Miss Robinson."

Back to Miss Robinson. I tried to take a few calm deep breaths. "But, when you think about it, it does actually look good for me."

Jackson looked up sharply. "How so, exactly?"

"Well, why would I be breaking into Bakermatic if I was guilty?" I masked my voice with a thick layer of boldness. "If I knew that I was guilty, why would I be so intent on trying to prove that Bakermatic did it? Why would I need to break in?"

Jackson shrugged. "To plant fake evidence? There are a hundred reasons why you could have broken in, Rachael, and not one of them makes you look less guilty."

I felt the ice run down my back. "I wasn't planting evidence."

Jackson stood up and placed his pen back in his breast pocket. "We'll see what the investigation turns up, Miss Robinson. I've got a detective down there sweeping the scene."

I gulped and subconsciously ran my hand along the front of my coat, where, nestled in behind the interior pocket, I had the paperwork I'd snatched just before

Simona walked in and caught us.

I hadn't planted any evidence, but I might have stolen some. Would the detective down on the scene know?

I shook my head to try to clear it and stood up. "So am I free to go?"

Jackson gave me a slow look up and down. "I can't hold you any longer. For now. But you'll have to go to court for those breaking and entering charges."

"Right."

"And Rachael," he said, showing me out the door, "I strongly advise that you stay out of trouble from this point forward. Or next time, I won't be able to let you go quite so easily."

Chapter 4

"Pippa!" I shook her shoulders as she woke, startled from a deep sleep. My sofa had become her new apartment following the recent eviction from her own.

"What? What is it?" As soon as Pippa opened her eyes, she groaned and slapped her head. "Rach, I just remembered what happened yesterday."

I jumped onto the sofa next to her, excitedly waving around a pile of papers. "Yeah, we got arrested. It was a real bummer."

"No, not that. I mean, I just remembered I got fired again."

"Pippa look at these. Hang on, what are you talking about, Pippa? You think the worst thing about yesterday was the fact that you got fired?"

She motioned to the sofa as she buried her face in a cushion. "Look at this, Rach! I'm sleeping on your sofa."

"And you can stay here for as long as you like," I pointed out. "Pips, did you think your job at Bakermatic was a serious thing?"

She rolled over, revealing her Teenage Mutant Ninja

turtles t-shirt she wore as a pajama top. "I mean, maybe it was stupid of me, but I thought I could actually stick it out there. The conditions were good, and I liked my manager—well, at least until she caught us breaking in."

My face fell. "Oh, Pips, I'm sorry. I never thought you were taking that job seriously." I swallowed. "But I'm sure the conditions weren't that good there. I mean, they take advantage of their employees, don't they? They are famous for giving out low pay and making their staff work overtime." At least, that's what I'd heard. That's what I'd assumed.

Pippa shrugged. "They paid a decent, livable wage..." She caught the look on my face. "It's okay, though, Rach, I know the only reason I took the job was to help you out. Like I said, I was just being silly, getting ahead of myself. Imagine me, actually able to hold down a job!" She let out a hollow laugh. "It was never going to happen."

I patted the sofa. "I mean it, Pips. You can stay here, free of charge, for as long as you like."

Pippa's face finally broke into a smile and she sat up. "So, what have you got there?"

I gulped, wondering now if it was such a good idea to tell her. She was clearly a little sensitive over the

Bakermatic issue. And I was still reeling from the news that it might actually be a halfway decent place to work. I tried to tell myself that Pippa just hadn't been there long enough to realize how terrible it really was. She only worked there a day! Any job can seem all right after only one day.

"Well, come on," Pippa begged, grabbing the papers out of my hands. "Oh," she said, her face falling when she saw the Bakermatic logo on top of the letterhead. "Where did you get these?"

I grimaced. "I swiped them before Simona caught us last night."

Pippa's mouth fell open and at first I thought she was going to give me a lecture, maybe throw the papers back in my face. But instead, her eyes began to twinkle with what looked like admiration.

"Good work, Rach."

"Phew, I thought you might be mad that I got you into even worse trouble."

Pippa laughed. "I've already been fired, how much worse can it be for me?"

"I guess that's true." I pointed to one of the documents. "Look at this, Pippa. It shows the kitchen cleaning log. It's where Bakermatic fills in all the health and safety details of the kitchen. For example, every night before closing, they need to check the temperature of the refrigerator, and they record everything in that log."

She frowned and read over the chart as she clutched it tightly in her small hands. "Yeah?" she said, confused. "This is what you were so excited about?"

"Look at the dates on it." I jabbed my finger.

"It's for the second week of October," Pippa said. "So?"

"So? What week is it now?"

Pippa screwed her face up in deep concentration. "I dunno? The second week of October? The first?"

I snatched the papers back from her. "It's the first week of October, Pips."

"I still don't see the big deal."

"Look at this log! They've already filled it in, in advance, for next week! How can they know the temperature of the refrigerators the week before? It's impossible."

Pippa slowly began to nod as she finally understood what I was saying. "So someone was clearly trying to save time."

"Cutting corners." I shook my head. "Typical of that place." I waved the papers in front of her. "If they don't even bother to make sure all the food is stored at safe temperatures, who knows what kind of stuff they are serving to customers!"

Pippa leaned back against the sofa and gave me a careful look. "I agree, it's a little dodgy that they did that. It's not right, but, Rach, it certainly doesn't prove anything."

"It proves that they don't take proper safety precautions. It proves they don't care about their customers. Pippa, I take a careful log every single day. I would never do my safety checks a week in advance like this."

Pippa looked away and didn't say anything for a long moment. "I know you wouldn't, Rach. But this is just one piece of paper. All it proves is that they cut corners on their paperwork this one week. It doesn't prove they don't care about their customers."

I could see the look in her eye. It was the same one Jackson had at the police station. She thought I was obsessed as well; I could tell.

I shuffled the papers in my lap. "I think I should take

these to the police."

"And where will you say you got them from, exactly?"

"They already know we broke in. What does it matter?"

"It matters because you were only charged with breaking and entering. You want a burglary charge as well?"

A smile threatened to take over my lips. It was very strange for Pippa to be the one giving me sensible advice. Was she right? Would handing this over to Jackson only get me in further trouble? After all, it wasn't the only thing I'd swiped.

But maybe it would finally make them investigate Bakermatic seriously.

"Come on," Pippa said, jumping up. "Don't you have a bakery to run?"

My mouth was agape. "Right now? No, I don't actually. I've got no customers. Hence, no business to run."

Pippa pulled a sweater on over her Turtles t-shirt. "Come on, you never know what today is going to bring! You don't know what you're going to find when you get to work."

I nodded. "You're right. I should at least go in. Are you coming with me?"

"I've got nothing else to do."

I wrapped my arm around her shoulders. "I'll have to pay you in cakes though, at least I've got plenty of those."

***

Pippa was right. I didn't know what I was going to find when I got to the bakery. What I didn't expect to find was the word "Killer" painted in bright red letters on the front window.

"Who did this?" Pippa asked as she took off her sweater and began to frantically mop up the paint. I noticed too late that it was actually my sweater she was wearing.

"Yuck." Pippa shook the sweater, the white of it now streaked with red, blood-looking paint. "This is kind of turning my stomach."

Even though she had managed to blur the word

"Killer" a little, it was still clearly legible.

"I think too much of the paint has already dried. Maybe we should have come in sooner."

I turned my key in the lock and shoved the door open. "Come inside, Pippa." On any other day, I would have been at the bakery at the break of dawn, getting the pastry rolled and mixing the muffin mixtures for the day. But the shelves were still brimming with the previous day's bake and I didn't feel particularly inspired to flush even more money down the toilet. But if I'd just come in, maybe I would have seen the person who'd sprayed that on my window.

Once the inside of the store, I didn't even bother to turn on the lights. If my bad reputation hadn't already been keeping the customers away, that word across my windows would have done the trick nicely.

I looked down at my hands and noticed that they were shaking.

"Rach," Pippa said, placing a hand on my shoulder. "Hey, it's not that bad. We can call a window washer to come get rid of the blood...I mean, paint." She pulled her hand away and gasped an apology when she realized she'd left a red hand print there.

"Don't worry about it," I said, shrugging it off. "And

don't worry about calling a window cleaner." I could hear the shake in my voice.

"It'll be okay."

I shook my head. "How? All I ever wanted to do was run this little bakery, make my own cakes and sell them to people. And I thought—just for a little while—that it was actually going to happen. But now, what's the point?"

Suddenly the door pushed open and a touristy looking woman with a large sun hat and sunglasses bustled in and began peering at the selection of cakes on offer. She nodded to herself with a look of appreciation on her face.

I straightened up. Perhaps she hadn't seen the paint on the windows. Racing behind the counter to tie my apron on, I asked her, "What can I do for you today, ma'am?"

She stood up straight. "I read online that this is the best boutique bakery in Belldale."

I nodded. At least the online reviews were still untarnished. I had the highest rated bakery in the area, with an average of 4.8 from over fifty reviewers. The kinds of tourists who check those sites always mentioned it when they came in.

"That's right," I said, gesturing to the still-full shelves of cakes and slices. "The best in town."

"Far better than that mass produced place down the road," the woman murmured.

"Bakermatic," I said, nodding. "Yes, of course, far better than them! They get most of their cakes pre-packaged from a factory. They are so chock-full of preservatives that they can last in their plastic packaging for months—maybe even years."

"Not these, though," the woman said, nodding at a row of Vanilla Slice. "You bake everything right here every day, don't you?"

"Well." I swallowed and looked over her shoulder at Pippa. "Yes, ma'am, everything is baked right here, on the premises."

"Fresh today?"

"Well...I...er. No, not today," I had to admit finally, seeing the woman's face fall into a pit of disgust.

"What do you mean, not today? Are these cakes fresh or not?"

"They are! They are only from yesterday, ma'am. They've all been refrigerated..."

She screwed her nose up. "And why haven't you

been baking today then? Why do you still have yesterday's cakes out for people to buy?"

I wanted to explain that, although not 100% ideal, that cakes baked only the day before were still fresh, and still a hundred times fresher than Bakermatic's atrocities. And more than that, I wanted to explain that I could hardly justify using hundreds of dollars of ingredients on cakes that were only going to end up in the trash. I hadn't even intended to open the bakery that day! But to explain all of that, I would have to explain why the store had been completely empty the day before.

Pippa stepped forward. "Rachael's just been a little sick, that's all."

I shook my head at her. I knew she was only trying to help, but that was the worst thing she could have said. Well, maybe the second worst.

The woman recoiled. "Well. I hardly wish to purchase cakes made by a sick woman, when those cakes aren't even fresh!" She cast an eye up towards the price list. "And at those prices! Why, miss, you have some nerve!" The woman turned on her heels and stormed out of the shop. She stopped as she saw the blurry blood red paint on the widows before hurrying away as though she'd seen a ghost.

I turned away. "There goes my good online rating."

"Come on," Pippa said, walking over to the door. "We're going to do something about this."

"Where are we going?"

She yanked the door open and stopped to stare at me. "Bakermatic."

***

The best thing we could come up with for disguises was the baseball visors and sunglasses that Pippa had in her bag.

"Pippa, if we get caught, there's gonna be big problems!"

"What are they gonna do? Call the cops again?"

I thought about Jackson's warning to me. "Yeah. They might."

"We better keep our heads down then," Pippa said as she pushed open the door into Bakermatic.

I cleared my throat. "Excuse me," I said to a young

wisp of a woman with blonde hair who was stacking muffins onto a stand.

"Yes?" she said nervously. Her name tag told me her name was Anna and that she was a trainee.

"Can you tell me, dear, are these muffins fresh?"

She shifted nervously. "I'll have to check with my manager."

"I'll take that as a no then. And can you tell me anything about your kitchen practices? Do you throw food out when it past its used by date? Do you keep a good temperature log? Or do you pretty much make it up as you go?"

"Rachael!" Pippa hissed as she pulled me away, leaving the tiny blonde girl wide-eyed on the other side of the counter. "You're going to give us away. She clearly doesn't know anything! She only started yesterday with me, she was one of the new recruits."

"Well, we can't leave yet. I need to catch them in the act." I looked over my shoulder covertly, hoping to see one of the new young employees drop a muffin and put it back on the shelf or something.

I walked back to the counter and, while Anna wasn't looking, I gently nudged one of the muffins onto the bench, cursing to myself when it teetered on the end of the counter without falling.

Anna spun around and cried out "Oh no!" before picking the muffin up.

"Oh, that's all right, just put it back on the stand," I said casually. "That's what you usually do, right?"

Anna shook her head. "No, they were very strict about this in training. If a cake falls off its stand, it goes straight in the trash. No risks get taken here, not when the health of our customers is at stake!"

"Right." My mouth was a thin line as Pippa pulled me away.

"I think we've stretched our luck far enough," she said. "Let's get out of here."

"Hey!" a loud voice bellowed. I recognized that one. "Not you two again! I'm calling the cops…again!"

There were murmurs and gasps from the full store as Pippa and I raced out the door before Simona could pull her phone out. She chased us and, just as I thought we were going to make it clear out the door, Simona reached out and slammed the door shut. "Uh-uh. You two aren't going anywhere."

Her hand still pressed the door shut above my head.

That's when I saw it. The palm of her hand, streaked with blood-red paint, faded in a clear attempt to get rid of it.

I turned slowly to Pippa. She'd seen it too.

"Go ahead, call the cops," I said, reaching up to pull Simona's hand away from the door. "But you're going to have to explain how this paint got on your hand."

Simona's cheeks turned as red as her hands. "I burned my palms on the oven," she muttered, pulling her sleeves down.

"Really? You want to tell the cops that when they arrest you for defacing property?"

Simona glared at us as Pippa yanked the door back, now that Simona had dropped her guard. "Come on, Rach, let's go!"

We sprinted the entire way back to the bakery, doubling over when we finally got through the doors. "I can't believe Simona did that to the window," Pippa said, breathless. "Why is she so hell bent on making sure you take the blame for Colleen's death?"

"Because, Pippa," I said, turning to look at her slowly. "I think Simona did it. That's why she doesn't want us snooping around, and that's why she is doing every thing she can to frame me. Now, all we've got to do is prove it."

Chapter 5

I told Pippa to go home and get some rest while I chucked all of yesterday's baked goods into the trash. It was a depressing enough task without a witness to add to my indignity.

Still, there was a little ray of hope beginning to dance in my stomach. Now I had a strong suspect. I was certain Simona had done it—the way her face had turned so red, the fact that she hadn't chased us, and the fact that the cops hadn't shown up at my door. Now, all I had to do was prove she was to blame and I could finally restore my reputation. I looked down at the rapidly filling bags of trash. *This is the last time I will ever throw out a day's work,* I vowed, dusting off my hands. Things were about to turn around; I could just feel it.

After filling four entire trash bags with cakes, slices of pie, donuts and pastries, I pulled the bags out into the alley, passing my stack of unopened mail from the day before. I'd been so distracted by Gavin that I hadn't actually finished opening the envelopes he'd passed me.

I dropped the trash bags and rummaged through the pile. My heart did a little flip when I saw that one of them was from the real estate compnay I leased the shop from.

I knew I was a little behind on the rent, but surely it couldn't be that bad. I ripped the envelope open and digested the contents of the letter.

My heart sunk to the bottom of my stomach and the room began to spin.

"EVICTION NOTICE."

"No... No..." I said, frantically reading the rest of the letter. I had one week to come up with the back rent or I was out of there.

"But I'm only a few weeks behind!" I wailed, throwing the letter down on the counter as I pulled my apron off, the straps suddenly so tight they felt as though they were blocking my air flow. But I knew the real estate company wouldn't care that I was only a few weeks behind. This was a high traffic street, prime real estate, and they'd have no problem finding a new business owner to take over the lease.

"I just hope they're not planning on opening a bakery here," I said bitterly, trying to fight back the tears. So much for things turning around. How was I going to find the back rent in just one week? Even if I could get Simona convicted before that and restore my reputation, it seemed totally impossible.

I glanced out the window. The lights at Bakermatic finally turned off for the night, and I could see Simona and her long dark ponytail creeping out into the night.

One week. One week to prove she did it and save my bakery.

***

Pippa was still dead to the world as I pulled my sneakers on the following morning. To be fair to her, I was up at the crack of dawn, my body still set to baker's hours even though I didn't have a bakery to attend to.

I smiled down at Pippa's sprawled out body as I passed her on the sofa. It would have been nice to have her on board for the day's task, but I knew that I could handle it myself.

The flyer from the street fair dangled from my hand. On it, a list of every single food vendor from the day that Colleen had died. If the cops weren't going to investigate thoroughly, then it was going to be up to me to speak to every last one of them.

There were fourteen different restaurants and cafes

that had stalls that day at the Belldale street fair. I decided to start with the one closest to my own bakery, a sandwich place called "Deena's Deli" run by a woman, called—you guessed it—Deena.

"Hey there, Rach," she said with a jolly grin. Deena was in her mid-forties with a golden blonde bob and somehow always managed to have flour on her shirt despite the fact that I wasn't sure what she actually baked with flour in her sandwich store. "What can I do for you today? Are you after a sandwich?"

Not at six in the morning, no. Deena opened early to catch the tradesmen on their way to work, looking for breakfast sandwiches filled with greasy bacon, sausage, and eggs. But that kind of thing so early in the morning churned my stomach.

"No, Deena, not today. They all smell delicious, though," I said, nodding towards the sizzling bacon concoctions flattened beneath the iron of the sandwich press.

Deena sighed. "Business has been a little slow this week." She lowered her voice and looked around as though she was about to say something forbidden. "You know, since the 'incident' at the street fair."

Hmm, so it wasn't just my shop that had been

affected, though I seemed to have been the worst hit. "Actually, Deena, that's what I wanted to talk to you about."

"You did?" Deena brushed her hands against her apron, leaving even more flour there. Where did it all come from? "Rachael, I know a lot of people are saying that you did it, but I just want to say, hand on my heart," She placed her hand against her chest in another cloud of flour, "that I don't believe you did it."

"I didn't do it. Deena, that's what I'm trying to clear up. Tell me, that day, did you see anything suspicious at all?"

Deena screwed her face up in great concentration. "Not that I can remember, dear. Oh, and I do wish I could help you. It's an awful shame what that man did to your window."

"Woman," I corrected her. "I already know who did it."

"Oh." Deena looked confused. "My mistake then, dear. I'm sure you know what you're talking about."

"I do." I cleared my throat and smiled. "So you really can't remember anything strange happening that day? Did you see the woman—the victim—Colleen Batters at all?"

"Ha!" Deena shook her head as she let out a hollow laugh. "She never deigned to stop by my stand, just like she always turned her nose up at my shop. Yet people are still avoiding my food this week. Just goes to show that she can have a negative impact after her death! I don't like to speak ill of the dead, Rachael, but that Colleen Batters was a real snob—a real piece of work."

I glanced around and noticed that the bacon sandwiches were burning. "You might want to check those." As she hobbled over, I watched Deena carefully. "So you didn't like Colleen then?"

Deena laughed again as she pulled out a charcoal sandwich and threw it in the trash with a sigh. "No one did, dear. That's why I keep saying: anyone could have done it; any one of the people running those stands could have wanted her dead." She turned to me with a hand on her hip. "Don't tell me you're in here accusing me of having something to do with it?"

"Deena, I'm just trying to get to the bottom of what happened. Eliminate suspects."

The jolly look had drained from her face. "What are you, a cop now?"

Although I already knew who had killed Coleen—or, at least, I was 99% sure—I still needed to make sure I was being thorough. Besides, I still needed the smoking gun, the proof that Simona had actually done it. And I could see that I was rubbing Deena the wrong way and if I didn't start to butter her up, she would likely kick me out of her store.

"Deena, I'm just trying to make my rent. You can appreciate that. I don't believe you killed Colleen. But can you remember seeing her eating anywhere in particular that day?"

Deena softened a little. She nodded. "Yes. She ate a fish pie from Carl's Fish Shop. I remember that clearly because she took joy in telling me how much better his savory selection was compared to mine."

"Sounds like Colleen." I patted the counter, sending flour flying. "Thanks, Deena. I'll let you get back to work."

***

"What are you talking about?" Carl said, pouring more water into his kitchen mixer. "Oh, darn!" he shouted. "Now I've gone and poured too much liquid into the darn pastry! You happy now?"

No! I certainly wasn't happy with the reception I'd gotten when I'd walked into Carl's Fish Shop. It seemed that he was another of the vendors who was hurting in the wake of Colleen's death, so I tried not to take his grumpiness too personally.

"That day at the Belldale Street fair," I said again, walking along the other side of the counter to follow him as he turned and threw battered fish into a deep fryer. "Do you remember serving a woman named Colleen Batters?"

He spun around. "You talking about the woman who died? Obviously I'd remember a thing like that. She never ate any of our fish, if that's what you're suggesting! Don't you think I've lost enough business as it is without people speculating even further, and without you coming in here and sticking your nose into other people's business?"

"Carl," I said, as calmly as possible. "I have a witness who says she did see Colleen eating one of your products, a fish pie, on the day in question."

He shook his head. "There's no way that's possible."

"How can you know that for sure? Did you keep track of every single person who ate from your stall that day?"

"Of course I did. Do you think I'd forget serving a woman that died?"

I sighed. "Why would Deena make that up?"

"Deena?" Carl said, leaning over the counter. "Oh, she's just trying to pass the blame! It was probably one of her bacon and egg sandwiches that killed the woman! After all, her food made me sick as a dog a few days ago." He stopped short all of a sudden.

I frowned. "When was this, Carl? When were you sick?"

He shrugged. "I don't know exactly," he muttered. "A few days ago." He picked up a washcloth and busied himself wiping a bench that was already sparkling clean.

"Three days ago?" I took a step closer to the counter. "Is that when you were sick?"

He shrugged. "I suppose so. It might have been."

"People don't forget getting food poisoning, Carl. Was it three days ago or not?"

He nodded.

"So, the day before the street fair." I raised an eyebrow and looked him up and down. "And yet, you were still able to get up in the morning and work a full shift at the Belldale street fair? A shift where you were so alert that you are able to remember every single customer you served?"

Carl just kept wiping the bench top. "I was feeling a little better once the morning rolled 'round."

"Carl. Be straight with me. You weren't at the street fair, were you?"

After a bit of hesitation, he shook his head. "No, miss, I wasn't there. I was so ill after eating one of Deena's contraptions that I was knocked out for two days straight. I just started feeling better today."

I sighed. "So why did you tell me you were at the fair?"

He shrugged again. "Because, if I wasn't there, how can I know for sure that Colleen didn't eat any of my food?" He shook his head. "But I know, miss, deep down, that it couldn't have been my food! I been here on this street for thirty years, miss. Why, this place is practically a local institution! And not once in thirty years have I ever made a single customer sick. I only have the best standards here. Unless the fish is fresh that day, I won't sell it."

I had always admired poor old Carl's commitment to freshness and quality. And I'd never heard anything bad about his store before. Any time I'd eaten from there myself, the food had always been piping hot, delicious, and never with an unpleasant super-fishy taste that some deep fried seafood gets. His batter was always golden brown, a result of regular oil changes. No wonder he was getting his back up. His thirty-year reputation was on the line.

"Carl, I know the possibility might be hard for you to fathom, especially with your high standards, but if you weren't there that day to supervise, anything could have happened."

"I don't care if I was there or not," he snapped. "I know what happened. It was Deena's food. It had to have been."

I sighed and tried to remain calm. "Carl, who did you leave in charge of the stall that day?"

He shook his head. "It was supposed to be the boy I get in to help me out on weekends, Tim, but he had some baseball game or something and couldn't be there for the whole day. He said he left the stall under the care of someone he'd found online. I can't even remember her name, to be honest with you."

"Her?"

Carl nodded. "That's about all I know of her. I didn't

even see her myself, but Tim said she was a real airhead." Carl stopped and looked up at me. "But that don't mean anything bad happened." Worry flashed in his eyes.

"It's okay, Carl. Do you remember any other details about her? Do you have a number, or an email address for her?"

He shook his head. "Tim was the one who posted the ad. Maybe he has more details for you. We just paid her cash on the day. She only worked for that one day, you see. Hey, you won't tell on me, will you, miss?"

I shook my head. Even though I made sure all my employees were paid by the book and got their regular breaks they were entitled to, Carl's slightly dodgy, under the counter payments were my last concern at that moment.

"So where is this Tim fella right now?" I dug my phone out of my coat pocket and opened the note app, ready to take down the address.

"Well, miss, he's actually gone back to college this week."

Great.

I sighed. "Do you have a phone number for him?"

74

Carl frowned and began to rummage though a stack of notebooks sitting beside the register. "I do somewhere, miss. Just give me a minute to find it."

"You don't have his number in your own cell phone?" I asked, growing impatient with his fumbling.

Carl shook his head. "I still use a landline, I'm sorry to say."

And I was sorry to hear it. "Look, maybe I'll come back later," I said, heading towards the door. "There's other people I need to talk to. If you could find Tim's number by the end of the day, that would be great."

"Wait, miss."

I paused, my hand about to push against the door. "What is it?"

"I do remember one thing Carl said about the girl who helped him that day."

I took a step back into the shop. "What do you remember about her?"

"I remember Tim talking about her hair, how it was a real crazy color. Bright red, and curly."

I swallowed. "Thank you, Carl," I whispered, hurrying to get out of there.

***

"Pippa?"

No answer. I stepped in the door and placed the keys back in my coat quietly. "Pippa?" I called out again softly.

There was an empty space on the sofa where she'd been, the imprint of her body bare, surrounded by empty takeaway containers and discarded drink bottles.

I sat down on the seat opposite.

Oh, Pippa.

I closed my eyes. *Come on, Rachael, it's important not to jump to conclusions. Just because the girl working with Tim had wild, red curly hair and was a little air-headed, it doesn't mean it was Pippa.*

And even if it was Pippa, it doesn't mean that she was the one who killed Colleen.

But if it was her, why didn't she tell me she was working at the fair that day? She knows how worried I've been! She saw the paint on the bakery window! How could she keep this from me?

I opened my eyes and looked at the mess Pippa had left on my sofa. Storming to the kitchen, I grabbed a trash bag and began to toss the items into it. *I let her sleep here, free of charge, and she can't even be bothered to tidy up after herself.*

One of the empty soda bottles rolled onto the floor and under the seat. I bent down to pick it up.

My hand felt something soft under there and I pulled it out, wondering what I could have left underneath there.

It was the visor that Pippa had taken off that night after the street fair, the one she'd thrown onto the ground right before we'd started to watch Criminal Point.

I turned it over slowly and looked at the writing embroidered on the front of it: "Carl's Fish Shop."

All the life drained out of me and I slumped down. So, she had been working for Carl's stand that day. I shut my eyes and tried to recall what had happened that night when Pippa had come in through the door.

I sighed. I told her I didn't want to talk about the day I'd had and then she'd thrown the visor off before I ever saw it. That might explain why she hadn't told me about her day working for Carl's Fish Shop.

But what about the day after that, and the day after that?

I'd sent her to spy on Bakermatic.

When all along, she might have been trying to cover her own tracks.

Oh, Pippa, what have you done?

I heard the sound of the front door opening and quickly shoved the visor back under the chair.

"Hey, Rach! Didn't think you'd be back already? How'd the sleuthing go? Did you find out who did it yet?"

Maybe.

I stood up and shook my head, barely able to look Pippa in the eye. "Not yet," I said quickly before hurrying towards the kitchen. Pippa followed me.

"Sorry about all the mess, Rach. I did intend to clean it up before you got home."

"It's fine." I shoved the trash bag in the can.

"Hey, is everything okay?" Pippa sounded worried. "You're not mad at me or anything, are you?"

I shook my head. I was still looking at the floor. "No. Why would you say that?" I finally dared to look at her.

Trying to gauge any flicker of guilt that might cross her face. "Why would I be annoyed at you, Pippa?"

She shrugged. "I don't know. You just seem weird. Oh well, if you say you're fine, I'll take your word for it. I'm gonna go watch some TV."

"Wait."

Pippa spun back around, her big blue eyes staring at me. Was there innocence in there? I couldn't bear to think that Pippa could be responsible for a woman's death.

She's always been irresponsible though. "Air-headed," that was the word Carl used. She easily could have used the wrong fish, not checked the used by dates, or left the fish sitting out in the sun. Anything could have happened with Pippa in charge.

"What is it, Rach?"

She batted her eyelids, long black fake lashes that framed the blue pools in between them. Pippa was air-headed, yes, but capable of killing a person? Even accidentally? No, not my best friend. She couldn't have.

And if she knew I suspected her, that could cause a rift between us that could never be mended again. Thirteen years of friendship down the drain.

"Nothing, Pips. Go and watch TV." I gave her a brave smile and she shot me an odd look as she turned around and headed back to the living room.

I stared down into the trash. I'd thought the only thing at stake was my bakery, and possibly my own reputation. I knew I was innocent. But could I say the same thing about Pippa? Now Pippa's freedom was at stake.

I didn't know if she was innocent. And if the cops found out that Pippa had been working at the fair that day, off the books, she was going to become a prime suspect. I knew how bad it looked for her. I didn't trust Detective Whitaker to go easy on her, or even to look at all the facts.

I tied up the bag and gave the can a little kick. Shaking my head, I realized that now, no matter how unglamorous the whole thing got, how unlike being a detective on TV it all was, I couldn't give up now. If Pippa was innocent then I was going to have to be the one to prove it.

Chapter 6

"Detective Whitaker, what are you doing here?"

"Can I come in?"

I took a step back into my house. It was difficult to make out the expression on Jackson's face in the dark of night, which, that evening, was not even lucky enough to be graced by the moon.

"What is this about?" I asked, pulling my sweater tighter around me. "Are you arresting me again?"

"I've never arrested you before," Jackson pointed out. "Simply questioned you."

"Yeah, well, it didn't feel that different from being arrested." I rubbed my arms against the autumn chill. "So you still haven't answered my question. Are you arresting me? Or just here for more questioning?"

Jackson clenched his jaw for a moment and for a second looked as though he was going to turn and leave. "I just wanted to check in on you. See if you were all right."

"All right?" I was stunned that he would just turn up

like this, to check on my wellbeing. There had to be some sort of a catch. "Are you on duty?"

He held his hands up. "This is all off the books."

"Hmm," I mused, looking him up and down. He was still in his expensive looking navy suit. "How can I be sure?"

He grinned at me. "You'll have to take my word for it." His smile faded once he saw that I wasn't returning it.

"Do you really think I'm all right?" I asked him. "After everything that's happened." *No thanks to you,* I wanted to add.

"Look, Rachael, I'm not here in a professional capacity. In fact, I really shouldn't be here at all." He glanced around furtively as though someone might be following him. "It's a clear conflict of interest. I just wanted to drop by and make sure you are okay." He took a step back. "I'm sorry. I should go. Forget I was even here."

"Wait," I said. "Do you want to come in for coffee or something?"

He hesitated, but I could tell from the way his eyes lit up that he did want to say yes. It was just going to take a little persuading on my part. Usually I could tempt people, men especially, inside with the promise of one of my cakes. I always had a spare batch lying around the house. But under the circumstances that was probably not the best tactic—especially if Jackson still thought I did it.

I narrowed my eyes. Perhaps this was the best way to figure out whether he still thought I was guilty, whether I was still a live suspect. "I've got a fresh batch of fudge brownies in the fridge," I said, checking carefully for his reaction.

No clear indication that he thinks he is going to die from taking a bite.

Jackson let out an uncomfortable laugh. "Are you trying to poison me?"

I just stared at him. "That isn't funny. Never mind." I tried to push the door shut, but he put his foot in the way.

"Sorry, I just meant that because I'm a cop, and...never mind. It was a bad joke. I don't think there's anything wrong with your cooking."

"Yeah?" I raised an eyebrow at him. "Come in and prove it then."

He glanced around covertly. Luckily for him, it was pure blackness out there and no one was going to see him sneaking into a potential murderer's apartment even if he had been followed. "I really shouldn't."

"Come on," I said, stepping back. "I'll heat them up for you. I promise you, these are the best brownies you will ever taste in your life."

"Well. Now *that* I do have to investigate."

Jackson followed me in and sat at the table while I warmed up a brownie for him. He sniffed the brownie and after I assured him there was no rat poison in the mixture, he finally took a bite.

"Mmm," he said, nodding. "Rachael, this is amazing. Just as good as the cake I sampled from your stand on the day of the fair."

I sat my coffee mug down with a bang.

"Sorry," Jackson said quickly, wiping the crumbs away from his mouth. "That was the wrong thing to say, wasn't it?"

"No. I mean, it wasn't exactly the best thing to say if you're trying to get back on my good side."

"I was in your good side at one stage?" he asked me with a mischievous grin. "Good to know."

"You know, you did eat one of my products that day," I pointed out. "And you didn't get sick, or die. I remember worrying at one stage that you might."

"You were worried."

I let out a large, over exaggerated sigh. "Can we just stick to the subject again, without any flirting going on?"

"I didn't know we were flirting. Are we flirting?"

"You're doing it again."

"Sorry."

I brushed my skirt down, playing with the hem for a moment. "I only meant to say, surely that must count in my favor as far as the investigation goes? Give me some brownie points, so to speak."

Jackson sat his brownie plate down, his face now dark and serious. "Rachael, you know I can't talk to you about any of this."

I swallowed. "Jackson, do you know what's happened to me since you brought me in for questioning?"

He looked down at the carpet. "Yes, I saw the paint on your shop window. That's partly why I dropped by here, even though I know I shouldn't have. I'm sorry, I've already said too much."

He stood to leave and I wanted to drag him back down onto the sofa. "Wait, Jackson. You don't have to go just yet, do you?"

"If I don't want to damage this case any more than I already have. Sorry, Rach. I just wanted to make sure you were still in one piece."

"Still in one piece?" I jumped up after him as he started heading out of the room. I grabbed him arm. "Jackson, what does that mean?"

He shook his head. "Nothing," he murmured. "Just meant, I wanted to make sure you weren't falling apart."

I raised an eyebrow and stuck my hand on my lip. "I don't fall apart quite that easily. It takes more than a little red paint."

"I really ought to go."

Jackson stopped talking as his eyes seemed to be transfixed by something behind me.

"What is it? What are you staring at?" I turned around and saw it. The red visor sticking out from underneath my designer chair.

Quickly, I stepped back and kicked the visor back under the chair. "You were just heading out?" I said to Jackson with the most casual tone I could muster, pushing him towards the front door. "Let me see you out. You better be careful out there tonight, it's pitch black and...and you're on a sugar high." I was rambling.

"What was that?" He stopped and I realized that my strength against his was nothing. I couldn't budge him.

"What was what?" Still as casual as can be.

"That object you just kicked under the chair." He placed a hand on my shoulder and gently but forcefully moved me out of the way.

"It's my private property, is what it is!"

But Jackson was already kneeling on the floor, inspecting the visor. "Just what I thought it was, the logo from Carl's Fish Shop."

Jackson turned to look at me with heavy eyelids. "Did you know this was here? Why do you have a visor from Carl's Fish Shop in your house?"

"I don't. I don't know how that got there."

Jackson stood up, the visor hanging from his hands, as though it was important evidence that he had to be careful not to dirty with his own fingerprints.

"Is this yours?"

I shook my head.

"Then why is it in your house?"

I put both hands on my hips. "What, I'm not allowed to have a visor from Carl's Fish Shop in my house? Why does it matter how it got there?" I took a step towards Jackson. "Unless, of course, Carl is a suspect in the Colleen Batters case."

Jackson's face clenched. "I told you not to do any more digging around. You need to be careful, or else..."

"Or else what?"

"You just need to be careful, Rachael!"

Jackson took a step back and rubbed his temples. "You need to tell me what this visor is doing in your home."

"I think you ought to leave. And you can drop that visor as well," I said, stomping towards the door.

"I can't just leave it, Rachael This is official police evidence now."

"I knew it!" I shouted, spinning around. "I knew you didn't just drop by for a casual chat, checking to see if I was okay."

Jackson looked hurt. "Rachael, I did, you have to believe that. It's just that I could hardly stop my mind from working on the case, could I? Especially when you are hiding evidence in your apartment."

I scoffed in offense. "I was hardly hiding evidence. I didn't even know that hat was there."

"Really?" Jackson asked. "Come on, Rach, do you really take me for a fool?"

"It was hidden under my chair," I said indignantly. "I never saw it till you pulled it out."

"Then I'm going to have to ask you to come down to the station with me again."

***

The night was so black I couldn't even see out the front of the car window until Jackson snapped the lights on, blinding me.

I sat back against the car seat and pressed my eyes shut. I didn't think I could stomach another trip to the police station.

"Last chance." Jackson turned the key in the ignition. "It can all end here, Rachael. Just tell me, why were you hiding that visor? Were you working with Carl that day?"

My eyes flew open. "No! You know I was too busy running my own stall!"

"You might have taken a break, helped him out for a while. You weren't exactly overwhelmed with customers that day."

I shook my head. "Real nice, Detective."

The ignition was still running, but we hadn't moved an inch.

"Who's that?" Jackson asked, pointing to the front of my apartment. "Who's going into your home?"

"No one," I said, trying to get his attention away from the red-haired figure, clearly slightly tipsy, trying to get her key to work in the front door. "Let's just get to the station. Come on, bring me in for questioning again."

Jackson flipped the engine off again so that we were in total silence as well as pitch-black darkness. He leaned forward, gripping the steering wheel as he watched Pippa struggle with the front door. "She's not breaking in, is she?"

"I don't know," I said, shrugging in an exaggerated manner.

"She clearly has a key." Jackson turned to me sharply. "I didn't know you had a roommate, Rachael."

"She's just staying with me temporarily."

Even though I could only see Jackson out of the corner of my eye, I could see him putting the pieces of the puzzle together, could see him figuring out how many lies I'd told him. Why did I feel so guilty about them? He was the enemy, after all. He was the reason I had "Killer" scrawled in blood-red paint over the front of my bakery. He was the reason I was about to get evicted from my shop.

Jackson tapped his fingers on the steering wheel. "So the visor belongs to your roommate."

I didn't say anything.

"What's her name?"

I still didn't say anything.

"Rachael, I'm going to find out with or without your help, so you may as well tell me. You might think you're helping your friend by staying silent, but believe me, you're not."

"Her name is Pippa," I said quietly.

"And was Pippa working for Carl's Fish on the day of the Belldale street fair?"

For some strange reason, in that moment I thought about poor old Carl, how I'd promised not to turn him in for paying Pippa under the table. Was he going to get into trouble now?

"Yes," I said finally. "She was working there. But Jackson—Detective Whitaker—you've got to believe me, *please*." I reached out and grabbed Jackson's arm. "You've got to believe me that Pippa had nothing to do with any of this."

Finally the clouds cleared a little and there was the slightest sliver of moonlight draping us. All I could see was Jackson staring back at me. "As I've told you numerous times before, Miss Robinson, you're going to have to leave the investigating to us. We'll decide how guilty or not this roommate of yours is." He picked up his radio and began to talk into it, giving his name and location to whoever was listening on the other end.

"Wait," I said, reaching out to try and stop him as Jackson glared at me. He switched off the radio for a moment.

"I won't hesitate to put you in cuffs if I have to, Miss Robinson."

"Please, just don't make that call yet. I can help you. I can help you solve this case. You don't need to involve Pippa in any of this."

Jackson shook his head in disbelief and scoffed as he

said, "How many times do I need to tell you..."

"I know, I know. Not to investigate. But you have to admit that I've done a better job than you have so far. You didn't even know about Pippa working for Carl, even though you've clearly already considered him as a suspect."

Jackson's face was stormy. I could tell I'd hit a nerve.

"Listen," I said, hurrying on, quickly trying to take advantage of the fact that I had him off balance. "I already know who did it, Jackson. The person, the woman, is named Simona. She works at Bakermatic down the road from my bakery. And she's trying to cover it up by making me look guilty. She's the one who painted "Killer" on my window."

Jackson frowned. "How do you know all this?"

"Because I investigated, of course. How else?"

Jackson rolled his eyes a little. "I mean, how do you know for a fact that she did it? Do you have proof? Proof that she killed Colleen? Proof that she vandalized your bakery?"

"Well, I have some pretty good evidence,"I said weakly. "She had red paint on her hands."

Jackson scoffed. "Didn't think so. See, that's the

difference between being an amateur sleuth and an actual detective, Rachael. You need to follow the cold, hard facts. Not decide who is guilty and then make the evidence fit it. We actually use our heads. Our brains. Not our personal prejudices."

I felt like a naughty school child who had just been chastised by a teacher. "I'm not prejudiced," I tried to protest.

"Oh please, Rachael. You have a personal grudge against Bakermatic that is clouding all of your judgment. You are so hell-bent on proving that they're guilty that you can't even see what's right in front of your face." Jackson pointed towards my apartment building. "Or what is right inside your own home."

I had fallen totally silent. I thought back to all the episodes of Criminal Points where one of the detectives had become too personally involved and been taken off the case. Did I need to take myself off the case? Had I just been screwed over so often by Bakermatic that I couldn't even take a step back and consider that someone else might be to blame?

I turned my face back to my apartment. Pippa had managed to find the light switch at long last and had plonked herself back onto my sofa.

Was I so close to Pippa that I couldn't see the worst in her? It was true that every time my brain even drifted towards the conclusion that she might be guilty it was as though there was an electric fence there that shocked me and wouldn't let me cross it.

"You're right," I murmured. "I've taken this case too personally."

Jackson let out a soft sigh. His reply was gentle. "It's okay, Rachael, you were just trying to protect your friend, and your bakery while you were at it. I can't fault you for that. You're a good friend, and a darn fine cook. But you'd better leave the detective work to those of us who are actually qualified."

"Can I get out of the car now?" I asked quietly.

Jackson nodded and I pressed the button to free my seatbelt.

Jackson was hot on my heels as we walked back to my front door, but I felt as though I was moving in slow motion.

"Are you going to arrest Pippa?" I asked him.

He gave me a reluctant smile. "Just bring her in for questioning."

I nodded. "You do what you need to do then."

Before I knew it, Pippa was being led out by Jackson, now Detective Whitaker again, as I kept my eyes fixed firmly to the floor, unable to make eye contact with her.

This is for the best, Rach. If Pippa did it then it's better for her—not to mention you—that she comes clean now. And it's better that you take a step back. Your interfering is only making matters worse.

But as I slumped down on the sofa, Pippa now taking my place in the police car, I couldn't quite manage to convince myself.

As I stared at the blank TV in front of me, I kept thinking about one thing.

You know those detectives on Criminal Point, the ones who got too close to the case, took it all too personally, and had to be removed? Most of the time, they ended up being right.

Chapter 7

"Pippa?" I called out gently, flicking on the light in the living room. Her spot on the sofa was empty.

Swallowing, I shuffled to the kitchen and boiled some water. I was going to need a strong cup of tea if I was going to get through the day that lay ahead. And I was going to need something solid in my stomach.

I opened the fridge. Apart from my plate of brownies, the only items in there were one solitary egg and a quarter of a carton of sour milk.

Brownies weren't going to cut it, and the milk may actually give *me* food poisoning. I slammed the door shut and grabbed my keys, deciding to risk it. I was going to have one of Deena's breakfast sandwiches.

I was trapped in line behind half a dozen tradesmen in overalls and woolen caps, waiting for their bacon and eggs and cups of Deena's terrible, burnt-tasting coffee.

At least her business seemed to have picked up.

I glanced over my shoulder at my bakery, the front of which was just visible outside the window. There was no one lining up to get in there.

"Rachael!" Deena said, beaming at me. "I'm so glad to see you. I didn't like how we left things yesterday."

I held my hands up in a show of mercy. "I'm just here for a breakfast sandwich," I said, nodding towards the sandwich press. "You got any double egg, single bacon sandwiches?"

She shook her head. "No, but I can make one for you."

"That would be great. Extra butter, please."

The rush of tradesmen ended as I leaned against the wall and yawned, keeping an eye on the press. Deena was watching me carefully and she kept opening her mouth and then shutting it again as if she was going to say something to me and then changed her mind.

"Hey, Rachael," she said, lowering her voice as she leaned in to whisper to me. "I was thinking about our conversation yesterday, when you were asking me all those questions about the street fair—and Colleen."

"Deena," I said, interrupting her. "I'm not sticking my nose into that anymore. I never should have in the first place. I apologize for asking you all those questions yesterday, it wasn't my place to do so."

"Oh." Deena's face fell a little. "It's just that..."

I pointed to the sandwich press. "That's burning, Deena."

"Oh!" She hopped over to the press and pulled out the sandwich. It was only a little charred on the sides but I could see that the eggs were now well done, while I prefer the yolk a little runny.

"Oh dear," Deena said. "I have a real habit of doing that."

"It's okay," I said, seeing her crestfallen face. "A little barbecue sauce will fix it up, if you've got some."

Out in front of the shop, I leaned against the wall for a moment, applying my sachet of barbecue sauce while some tradesmen—painters, by the looks of their overalls—loitered beside me.

"She's always burning these darn things," one of them complained, a younger man in pale blue overalls, who shook his head.

"Come on, man, give her a break. She's been having a tough time ever since that woman left those awful reviews online. It really ruined her business."

"Excuse me," I said, butting in. I gave both the men my biggest, cheesiest grin. "Sorry, I couldn't help overhearing. I think Deena's food is great, some of the best I've ever eaten!" A lie. "I can't imagine why someone would ever give her a bad review. When was this?"

The younger man shrugged. "It was about a month or so back now, a bunch of really bad reviews in a row, but Deena reckons they were all from the same woman. Some woman with a grudge against her."

"Do you happen to know the woman's name?" I asked, trying not to sound too eager to know the answer.

"Sorry, love, no idea." Both men chucked their half-eaten sandwiches into the trash before strolling off to their waiting van, leaving me to wonder: did I really need to butt out of this case? Or was overhearing this a sign that I should ignore Jackson, and follow my own gut after all?

***

There were several review sites online that the men could have been talking about, but by far the most popular, and influential, was Trip Advisor—the same site that brought me my floods of tourists. Or, used to, anyway.

But it had been a while since I'd scoped out the reviews of my local competitors. Back when I'd first opened the bakery, I used to spend hours every day getting lost in all the reviews—checking my own, checking Bakermatic's, then checking for any recent reviews for the other restaurants and cafes near the bakery, making sure my ranking hadn't slipped. But I soon figured out that it was a giant time suck, and that my time could be better spent improving my own baking, my own recipes, and my own business.

So it must have been at least two or three months since I'd even looked at the reviews for Deena's Sandwiches.

Frowning, I sat down in front of my laptop with another strong cup of tea and saw that Deena's average rating had dropped to 2.1 out of 5. Ouch. Last time I'd checked, it had been at least a 4. What on earth had happened?

Scrolling down, I quickly got my answer. There was a spate of reviews all from the same week, all with very similar comments, all giving Deena's Sandwiches 1 star out of 5. Even though all the reviews had different usernames besides them, it was clear from the wording and the fact that the same complaints kept being repeated over and over again that this was one person operating under a dozen different sock puppet accounts.

"The worst food I have ever tasted in my life!"

"This food made me sick to my stomach. I have been throwing up for the past 48 hours!"

"Never eat here! That is a warning that you dismiss at your own peril."

I sat back and thought about Carl getting sick from one of Deena's sandwiches earlier that week. I was grateful now that I'd thrown my sandwich in the bin after a few bites of the rubbery egg and burned bacon.

But was this person telling the truth? Had Deena's food really made them sick? Or were they just trying to slander Deena's name and reputation?

There was no picture next to the usernames and every time I clicked on the username, it always showed that the 'reviewer' had only left the one review. It was clearly someone who wanted to remain anonymous. It was also someone who was clearly nasty and had a vendetta out against Deena's shop. Someone antagonistic enough to come back again and again, who wanted Deena, and everyone else, to know just how unhappy they were.

And I knew just the kind of person who would do that.

Colleen Batters.

***

The door opened and then closed with an angry thud, causing me to jump out of my seat.

"Pippa, come and have a look at this! Come look what I've found out."

I could hear Pippa throw her keys down on the bench before she slowly walked into the spare room I used as an office. She had a scowl on her mouth and a face like thunder.

"What have you found?" she asked in a low growl. Far from the usual perky, high-pitched voice she normally used.

"Pippa, what's wrong?"

She let out a snort of disbelief. "What the heck do you think is wrong? I've been down at the police station, Rachael! They think I gave Colleen the fish pie that killed her! And where have you been all day?"

"Sleuthing" I said with smile, attempting to put her in a good mood. "I was on my way to the station to find you, really I was, but then I stumbled across this new information. Pippa, where are you going?"

She stormed out of the room as I chased after her. "Pippa, please, don't be like this!"

She spun around. "How do you expect me to be, Rachael?! You're the one who told that detective that I was working at Carl's that day! How could you?"

I held my hand up. "Hey. You're the one who kept that from me, Pippa. I'm the one who ought to be mad at you! You knew I was being blamed for Colleen's death, and you kept this from me? When it could have helped me?"

Pippa looked away as the anger drained from her face slightly. "That night when I got home, you didn't want to talk about it," she mumbled. "Besides, I wasn't supposed to go mouthing off about it or Carl could get into trouble. I know how seriously you take proper business procedures. I knew you'd ask me if I got paid properly, if I got my regular meal breaks."

I sighed. "Fine. Whatever Pippa. So you're telling me that you didn't keep quiet because you knew you might be a suspect?"

Guilt crept onto Pippa's face. "I dunno, Rach. Maybe." Her head was still hanging, like a puppy that has been scolded for going to the bathroom on the kitchen floor. "I'm sorry, I should have been honest with you, I should have told you I was there." She lifted her head and I saw how tired her eyes were. "But I honestly didn't see anything that day that could have helped."

"Think, Pips. You didn't see Colleen Batters at all? There are witnesses who saw her eating a fish pie from your stall."

Pippa rolled her eyes. "You sound like the cops. I don't even know what this Colleen Batters looks like! Maybe I served her, maybe I didn't." Pippa threw her hands up in the air. "Who knows!"

"It's okay," I said, patting her arm. "Don't worry about that now. I'll get you some tea."

"But I am worried about it, Rachael. The cops think I'm guilty."

"They think everyone is guilty," I pointed out. "That's their job. Look, I've got something that might make you feel a little better."

"You do?"

"Follow me."

Pippa flopped down on the bed in the spare room after she'd read through all the reviews and I told her what I'd overheard about Deena. "Don't you see, Pips? Deena had the perfect motive to murder Colleen. She was ruining her business."

Pippa sat up. "Yeah, but she said Colleen didn't eat from her stall that day."

"Of course she would say that. But she's been losing business for months, not just this week like the rest of us. Sure, she's been a little hurt by Bakermatic, but..."

Pippa let out a little laugh.

"What?"

"It's just the first time I've heard you mention Bakermatic in a while. Usually you're obsessed with them. Are you finally willing to admit that they may not be the bad guys?"

"Hey, they're still the bad guys. Let me be very clear on that. But maybe Jackson was right. Detective Whitaker, I mean. Maybe I was too focused, too biased. Now that I've taken a step back, I think the real suspect has become a lot more obvious."

Chapter 8

"Can I speak to Detective Whitaker, please?"

"He's not at the station right now," a bored voice on the other end of the line said. "Is this an emergency?"

"Not exactly an emergency."

"Well, is it or isn't it?"

"I'll call back later."

Pippa was looking at me expectantly as I ended the call. "What happened?"

"He's not there." I let out a sigh. "Even if he was, I don't think he'd want to listen to anything I have to say. He thinks I'm obsessed with blaming Bakermatic. He probably won't even listen to my new theory now. I'm like the girl who cried wolf."

"Well, you *were* a little obsessed with Bakermatic," Pippa said teasingly.

"I know. And look, I still haven't completely crossed them off my list. But, if Deena is to blame, then I'm willing to accept that. I still think Bakermatic should be closed down, though."

"Come on," Pippa said, grabbing my arm. "Speaking of the devil, I need to go down there to pick up my paycheck from the day I worked there. And you're coming with me."

Despite my groans and protests, I somehow managed to end up in front of Bakermatic's sickly yellow shop front. "I'm not coming inside, though," I insisted, arms crossed.

"Yes, you are," Pippa said. "Come on, I don't want to face Simona on my own. You owe me at least this, Rachael."

I sighed. "Fine. Let's just get this over with."

Expecting to have to wade through an avalanche of customers, like usual, I was shocked to find that Bakermatic was almost empty, like a pastel yellow desert. "What's going on?" I spun around as Pippa shrugged at me.

"Haven't you heard?" Both Pippa and I stopped at the sound of Simona's voice. She was holding a broom, clutching it like it was a weapon and we were her prey. "Word's got out that Colleen's death was no accident. She was poisoned." Simona banged the broom on the ground and began a slow, angry sweep. "So I guess that means we're all screwed now." She shot me a low scowl.

"No thanks to you."

"No thanks to me?" I asked. "You're the one who has been trying to make me look guilty!"

"Because you are," she snapped, holding the broom up straight as anger flashed in her eyes. "I'm going to lose my job if things don't pick up," she said, taking an ominous step towards me.

"Maybe we should leave," Pippa whispered, tugging at my sleeve.

"Yeah, you ought to," Simona snapped. "Before I call the cops on you."

"No," I said firmly. "Pippa needs her money. We're not leaving until we get it."

Simona let out a laugh that was so giddy it almost amounted to a giggle. "What, for that one day you managed to last here, before you screwed it up?"

"Yes," Pippa said, crossing her arms. "I worked for that money, and maybe it would be cool if I was rich enough to just let it go. Believe me, I certainly never wanted to see your face again, but I need that hundred bucks."

Simona shrugged and dropped the broom. "Whatever. Wait here while I go to my office."

"Well, this is humiliating," Pippa said as we waited for Simona to come back with the paycheck.

"At least we get to see Bakermatic empty of customers," I pointed out. "I'm quite enjoying the sight."

"Rachael, look," Pippa said, grabbing my arms. She spun me around so that I was looking out the window.

"What the heck is Deena doing?" I asked, crouching down a little so that I was out of her line of sight should she look around. "Pippa, get down," I whispered, pulling her after me.

We both watched as Deena crept up to the front of Carl's Fish shop and glanced around before pressing her face against the glass of the window.

"What is she looking for?"

I shook my head. "She's probably heard the news that Colleen's death was no accident and realizes it's only a matter of time before she is arrested. She's probably getting desperate."

Carl came rushing out of his shop, startling Deena, and they had an argument before she scurried off, leaving a puff of flour in her wake.

"What are you two doing?"

Pippa and I both bumped our heads on the table as

we jumped up at the sound of Simona's voice.

"Still creeping around, I see." Simona held the check towards Pippa and told us to get out.

"Why?" Pippa said. "You don't seem exactly rushed off your feet with customers."

As I saw Simona's face fall, I actually felt kind of bad for her. I understood the feeling, and even though Simona didn't own Bakermatic (she would have been quite far down the food chain in the grand scheme of things) it still sucked to feel responsible for a business that was failing.

"Hey," I said to Pippa gently. "Don't go rubbing it in."

Simona looked up at me in surprise. "I thought you'd be the first to revel in this business's failures." A note of bitterness crept into her voice. "I thought you'd be dancing on our graves."

"I just know how it feels, that's all." I sighed. "If I did have anything to do with it., well, I'm sorry."

Pippa's mouth was wide open.

Simona held my gaze for a long moment then shrugged. "It's not just you," she admitted. "In fact, it's not just the Colleen Batters thing either. We had all these bad reviews on line in the past couple of days, saying that our food made all these people sick."

Pippa and I turned and looked at each other.

"Hang on," I said. "What do you mean, 'all these people'?"

Simona frowned. "There's a bunch of different reviewers. But they're all saying the same thing."

"Do you have a computer in here? Can I take a look at it?" I asked, already walking towards Simona's office. I knew where it was, after all.

"Er, sure," Simona said, chasing after me.

"Here we go." Simona pointed over my shoulder as she showed me all the reviews on Trip Advisor.

"Oh my gosh," I said, glancing over the comments.

"Stay away from this place!"

"Ignore my warnings at your own peril!"

"This place will make you sick—or worse!"

The same syntax as the reviews left on Deena's Sandwiches all those months ago.

All the user reviews had been posted in the past two days. I turned to face Pippa. "Don't you see, Pippa? These were all posted this week. Meaning, after Colleen died."

Pippa nodded, a grave look coming over her face. "That means they can't have been posted by Colleen."

"And neither could those comments on Deena's Sandwiches. Colleen isn't the mystery reviewer."

There was a flash of dread in Pippa's eyes. "Then who is?"

***

"Come on," Pippa said, "You can call Detective Handsome later. It's not like you've got anything solid to tell him anyway."

"But I'm starting to piece this all together, Pippa. I think I should tell him what I've learned." I pulled my phone out of my pocket and began tapping in the number for the Belldale Police Station again.

"It can wait five minutes, can't it?" Pippa asked as we crossed the road. "I need you for moral support again when we go to Carl's."

"What for?" I asked, pulling the phone away from my ear. "Didn't you get paid by him already? It was cash under the table, right?"

Pippa nodded a little as she rolled her eyes. "Yeah, but he only had half the cash for me that day and told me to drop by any time and collect the rest. I've been putting it off because of everything that happened, wondering if he'd throw it in my face if he saw me again!" She took a deep breath. "But I'm feeling brave since I faced Simona, so I'm gonna do it now!"

I nodded. "Right you are, Pips. You should get what you're owed. Let's go!" I said brightly, pushing the door open to Carl's, expecting to find another wasteland. But the place was bustling with customers and Pippa and I had to squeeze past them as we tried to make our way to the counter.

"Hey, no cutting!" one angry young man with a sleeve of tattoos yelled at us.

"We're not cutting in line!" I said back to him. "We're not ordering any food, just calm down."

He scoffed. "Well, you ought to, it's the only place around here that's safe to eat at."

Carl's eyebrows shot up as he saw Pippa approaching the counter. "What are you doing here?" he scowled.

"I need the thirty bucks you owe me from the street fair," Pippa said boldly.

Carl shook his head. "You've got some nerve coming in asking for that."

"If you don't give it to me then I'll have to tell the authorities that you paid me off the books that day." She nodded towards the rest of the staff. "And that you avoid paying taxes on your regular employees' wages as well."

Carl scowled at her. "Well, I'm run off my feet here at the moment, missy. You're going to have to go out the back and wait."

"Can't you just take it out of the till?"

"Out the back!"

Pippa sighed and I told her it was okay as we stepped out the back door to wait until the rush was over. There was a strong fishy smell in the lane and I wished we'd just left and come back later. But I knew that Pippa might not have the nerve to come back again if we left now.

I tried to ignore the smell, bopping up and down a little to try and keep warm. I took my phone out of my pocket.

According to the receptionist, Jackson still wasn't at the police station. I sighed and asked if I could leave a message then. "Tell him to please call Rachael Robinson back. No, I don't want to leave any further details. Thank you." I shivered and shoved the phone away again.

Still no sign of Carl.

"Why didn't Carl have the money to pay you the other day anyway?" I asked Pippa.

Pippa titled her head. "Apparently, the business has been suffering for a long while. They were a bit strapped for cash that day and they'd only be able to pay me half of it. I mean, whatever, I needed the job so I didn't argue with them." Pippa started hopping from foot to foot. "I hope he's actually going to give me the cash today."

I nodded towards the full shop. "Doesn't look like he has a problem with cash right now. I think you'll be fine."

Pippa let out a short laugh. "Yeah, he seems to be the only shop on the street who doesn't have a problem with bad reviews."

Pippa stopped talking as we stared at each other.

"Pippa," I said, realizing something. "How come Carl recognized you when you came into the shop?"

"What do you mean? I've met him before. At the street fair. He's the one who told me to come and collect the cash!"

I swallowed. "He told me he wasn't at the street fair. That he'd been suffering food poisoning after eating one of Deena's sandwiches."

Pippa let out a little laugh of disbelief. "I don't think anyone could ever get sick from one of Deena's sandwiches! She overcooks them all to the point that not even the strongest of bacteria would be able to survive!"

"You're right," I murmured. "Yet she got all those bad reviews a few months ago."

I glanced over my shoulder at Carl, who was eyeing us carefully. "Pippa, I think we ought to get out of here," I said, pulling her towards the door.

"What? Why? I need to get my cash."

"We have to go," I whispered to her. "Deena isn't the one who killed Colleen. And her food's never made anyone sick, unless they are allergic to charcoal."

"What are you saying, Rachael?"

I kept one eye steady on Carl as I began to plan our escape. "I'm saying, Pippa, that we need to get out of here, right now! Or losing thirty bucks is going to be the least of your problems, or mine."

Chapter 9

The back door slammed shut behind Carl as he stomped into the alleyway after us. The stench of fish had become almost unbearable.

"Just where are you two going then?" Carl asked us, focusing first on me, then on Pippa. "Don't you want your money?"

Pippa clutched her purse close to her as she took a step backwards. "Um, no you know what, I just realized that there's somewhere else I really need to be. I can come back for the money some other time, since you're so busy." She tried to step in front of Carl as he cut her off. He was a bull now and Pippa was the red flag. I could practically see his nostrils flaring as he closed in on poor Pippa, who was inching closer and closer towards the brick wall of the alley.

Carl kept switching his gaze between Pippa and me. "I didn't realize you two were so cozy," he growled menacingly. "This certainly makes things interesting."

At the last moment before she was about to hit the wall, Pippa tripped over a box of old discarded fish guts and bones, shrieking as she went over backwards, her backside landing in the pungent materials.

"Pippa!" I ran over to her but Carl grabbed me by the collar of my peacoat. "I think you girls better come with me." He reached down and snatched Pippa up as well, dragging us both to what looked like a small shed at the end of the alley.

He stopped before he reached the door and I thought for a moment that we were saved, that he had realized that throwing two young women into a shed was insane. "Carl, please, this is only going to make things worse for you," I reasoned with him, thinking he already knew that and he was ready to agree and let us go.

But instead, he reached into my coat pocket and grabbed my phone.

"Yours too," he said to Pippa, holding out his hand as she placed her cell there with trembling fingers.

"Get in here!" Carl said, shoving us into the small building with a strength I'd never have guessed he possessed. He shut the door and suddenly we were engulfed in darkness.

"Hey!" Pippa said, banging on the wooden door. "What do you think you're doing?"

Carl's muffled voice travelled through from the other side of the door. "I'm making sure you can't cause any more trouble! Or talk to the cops. Ever again."

We heard the sound of a lock turning and then Carl's footsteps walking away.

"Help us!" Pippa called out, banging on the door. "Carl, you can't keep us in here!"

"It's no use," another voice called out, causing Pippa and I to both jump out of our skins.

"Deena?" I asked, squinting in the dark. If only Carl hadn't taken our phones, we might have had a flashlight.

And a way to phone for help.

I heard Deena groan and as my eyes adjusted, I could see that she was bleeding from a cut on the top of her head, blood inching towards her eyes. "My gosh, Deena, what did Carl do to you?"

"Nothing," Deena said, shaking her head. "Well, he threw me in here, so not exactly nothing, but I hit my head once I was already in here. I can't see a darn thing since Carl took my phone!"

"But why did he lock you in here?" Pippa asked.

Deena shook her head again. "I was just coming by to get some money that Carl owed me."

I heard Pippa let out a scoff.

"But he didn't answer the front door, so I pressed my face up against the window," Deena continued. "That's when I saw him, on his laptop, and guess what he was doing?"

I shook my head and tried to catch Pippa's eye in the dark. "I don't think we need to guess," I said. "Writing bad reviews?"

Deena nodded. "Writing a bad review of *my* shop, no less. I thought those days of a hundred one star reviews were all behind me! Business had just started to pick up again! I thought it was a disgruntled customer who'd made all those reviews. I never in a million years would have thought a competitor was writing them!"

"You're too trusting, Deena," I told her. "What happened after Carl saw you?"

"He came running out the door after me, chasing me down the street."

I sighed. "We saw the argument from Bakermatic," I told her. "Sorry, Deena, I never thought he would lock you up. I thought it was just a simple argument amongst neighbors."

"You don't have to apologize. We're all in the same

boat now, after all. But, Rachael, my dear! What are we going to do?" Now that my eyes had adjusted to the darkness, I could see the terror forming in Deena's. "Is he going to do to us what he did to Colleen?"

I gulped. "Not if I have anything to do about it," I told her with a confidence I didn't actually feel.

***

Pippa leaned against the wall, knocking over a mop that had been standing upright against it.

"I can't believe this is happening," Pippa said. "Rach, how long do we have before Carl comes back for us?"

I loved that she thought I knew. "Let's just hope that rush hour in the shop lasts a little longer."

I glanced over at Deena, who was slumped against the floor. "Deena?" I knelt down and give her a gentle tap on the face. "Deena, you need to keep your eyes open! You need to stay awake!" I looked up at Pippa. "We need to get her out of here."

"We all need to get of here," Pippa pointed out. "Or we're all dead."

I checked Deena's pulse before I stood up. She was still alive—for now. "Well, you got any ideas?"

She didn't answer. "Pippa?"

"Sorry, Rachael. I was just thinking about something that happened on the day of the fair. Oh, Rachael, this is all my fault," Pippa whispered.

"Pippa, what are you talking about?"

"I didn't think anything of it at the time," Pippa said, her voice getting more high pitched with every word. "I thought we were just innocently chatting."

"Pippa, just tell me what you did."

Pippa gulped. "It's just that we weren't selling many products and Carl started grumbling that Bakermatic was taking all the customers from all the other stalls with their free promo giveaways."

"Well, they were," I said with some indignation, before I realized I was defending a killer. "Go on."

"So I mentioned that it seemed like everyone hated Bakermatic and I sorta mentioned that you did specifically, considering that you sell almost the same products," Pippa said. "Oh my goodness, Rachael, I'm so sorry. I didn't say we were close friends or anything, but I was telling Carl about how Bakermatic was stealing all your customers and undercutting your prices, and that you were having trouble making rent."

I sighed. I think I could see what happened next. "It's okay, Pippa," I tried to say.

She kept talking. "Carl was listening really intently, kept saying, 'well, isn't that interesting.' Then a woman walked by with a piece of your cherry pie in her hand. I recognized it, of course, as it's my favorite. It might have been Colleen Batters. I never met the woman before! But she threw your cake away before she'd even had a bite. I remember thinking that was very rude. And then Carl quickly asked me to take the trash over to one of the dumpsters, like he was trying to get rid of me. I remember being put out by the request because I wanted to tell the woman off for throwing one of your cakes away."

"So you didn't see what happened next?"

Pippa frowned, deep in concentration. "Once I'd returned back from the dumpster, she was already gone." Pippa suddenly gasped. "But I do remember him grinning like a lunatic afterwards, and, Rachael, that's when he took off. I never saw him again after that for the rest of the day."

"Hmm, must be when he got 'sick'," I said, putting

finger quotes around the 'sick' despite the fact that it was too dark for Pippa to see me properly.

Pippa's voice was full of guilt. "I'm sorry, Rachael. He must have heard me talking about you and Bakermatic and decided to take advantage of the fact that Colleen had one of your pies, knowing that you were under stress financially and would be one of the top suspects. I didn't know that she was Colleen Batters, the woman who had been making all your lives hell."

"She did annoy all of us, that's true," I said. "But I never wanted to kill Colleen! Well, I suppose sometimes I *did*, but I never would have actually done it. I'm sure Deena felt the same way."

A groaning sound came from the ground and I was relieved to discover that Deena was still conscious. "Carl was in deep debt," she said, trying to sit up.

"Deena, don't move suddenly," I scolded her. "Just hold tight until..."

"Until what?" Pippa whispered. "How are we going to get out of here?"

Deena didn't heed my warning and kept talking. "He was getting more and more desperate all the time, cutting corners, not paying staff properly, even borrowing money from me, as I told you." Deena pulled herself to her feet. "A few months ago, when things were really bad for him, he agreed to do an interview for Colleen's food blog."

I rolled my eyes. I remembered Colleen's promise to review my black forest on her blog. I guess that never happened.

"She promised Carl that it was going to be a positive review, but then she ripped him apart, gave him one star, and things just got worse for Carl from there on." Deena let out a loud sigh. "I thought it was Carl I saw painting 'Killer' on your store front. I couldn't be sure, but I did think it was him at the time."

"That's why you said 'he' when we were talking about it," I said, realizing.

"Rachael, all of this is what I was trying to tell you when you came to see me yesterday. But you said you'd given up investigating."

"So he decided the best way to right his business was to follow Colleen's lead and give every business in the area a bunch of bad reviews. And then, when the opportunity presented itself to get revenge on Colleen, I guess he took it. I'm sorry, Deena. I should have listened to you. Maybe I'm not so great at this detective stuff after all."

Deena shook her head. "No, you *are* good at it. You figured out it was Carl, even without my help. You just shouldn't have stopped, that was the problem."

Pippa reached out and gripped my arm. "Rach, can you hear that?"

I nodded. "Footsteps."

I glanced around the closet. "Okay, you take this," I said to Pippa, handing her a block of wood.

"What are you going to take?" Pippa asked frantically.

I took off my red peacoat. "I'll wrap this around his neck, and you hit him with that. You ready?"

"No?!"

The lock turned swiftly and suddenly bright sunlight streamed into my eyes as I stumbled back into the closet, blindly throwing my coat at the body there. "Go on, Pippa, hit him!" I shouted.

"I wouldn't do that if I was you, ma'am," a deep voice boomed. "Or you'll be guilty of assaulting a police officer."

"Jackson?" My eyes adjusted to the sunlight and I threw my arms around his neck as Pippa looked on with her mouth wide open.

"Ahem, sorry," I said, pulling away. "Not sure what came over me then. I'm just glad to see you Jackson—I mean, Detective Whitaker—I'm really glad to see you right now."

He grinned at me. "It's okay, 'Jackson' is fine under the circumstances. Are you ladies all right?"

I stood back and allowed him to take a look at Deena, while Pippa and I were helped outside by a pair of uniformed police officers.

"I got your message," Jackson said once he'd finished with Deena. "I knew something was wrong. I tried your bakery first, then Bakermatic, then they told me you'd come here. One of the customers told us that they'd seen Carl pulling you and Pippa down the alleyway. But we didn't know about Deena."

I glanced over my shoulder as one of the paramedics attended to Deena. "I'm sure glad she's okay," I mentioned to Jackson, as he reached over to adjust the blanket on my shoulders, which someone must have given me at some point.

"I have to admit, I'm glad you're okay," Jackson said. "We've suspected Carl right from the start and when I saw that paint on your bakery the other day."

"I know, I know," I said. "Carl did it. That's why you

came to check on me. You thought I was in danger."

Jackson nodded. Checking first that no one was watching, he reached out and gently squeezed my arm. "That's why I told you to stop snooping around. To let us do our jobs. Not because I didn't think you were any good at it, but because this is exactly what I was worried would happen."

I looked up at him. "I assume you've arrested Carl. But do you know that he was writing fake reviews for all the businesses in this neighborhood? About the fact he underpays his employees, or doesn't pay them at all?"

Jackson shook his head. "No, we didn't know about any of that. I have to admit, your snooping will help put him away. Not to mention the fact that we can get him on a bunch of other charges now." Jackson raised an eyebrow.

I smiled at him. "When do you get off duty, Jackson? Can I perhaps interest you in another one of my brownies?"

Jackson looked over his shoulder again before turning back to me. "Sounds great, and I would love to sample one of your many treats, but I'm afraid, for the time being, that will have to be as a customer only—at least until this case is wrapped up. I hope I can trust you not to get involved in any police matters in the future, Miss Robinson."

Jackson shot me a wink before he began to walk away.

"I can't quite go promising that just yet, Detective Whitaker," I said quietly, once I was sure he was out of earshot.

I walked back over to Pippa, who was standing there, grinning at me from ear to ear.

"What was that all about?" she asked, punching me in the arm.

"I don't know what you're talking about," I replied coyly.

Pippa laughed and grabbed my shoulders, looking me square in the face. "You get in a lot of trouble, Rachael. Are you sure you want a cop following you around on a regular basis?"

She was right. But maybe it wouldn't be so bad if that cop was Jackson Whitaker.

Epilogue

I cleared my throat. "Ahem. I would like to welcome to Rachael's Boutique Bakery, our newest member of staff: Pippa McDonald!"

I clapped as Pippa spun around and bowed to the crowd of one. Placing the pink apron over her head proudly, I said, "I can finally afford to have an employee, now that business is booming again. And I couldn't be more pleased that my first employee is my best friend in the whole world."

The smile on Pippa's face faded a little. "Oh, Rach, are you sure? I hope I don't screw things up for you."

I placed my hands on Pippa's shoulders. "You're going to do fine."

We both spun around as a person wearing a yellow polyester shirt walked sheepishly through the door. "I just wanted to wish you guys good luck on your reopening," Simona said, before pulling something out from behind her back.

She handed me the basket of muffins. "It's a good will gesture," she explained. "I was hoping in the future our stores could work together, rather than competing all the time. After all, you did help to clear our name as well. And you got all those fake negative reviews removed from online."

I smiled at her. Even though I had no intention of eating those prepackaged cakes, I did appreciate her extending the olive branch.

She turned to face Pippa. "And Pippa, even though you were a terrible employee, I wish you good luck in your new job." Simona shot me a look before she walked out the door. "You too. You're gonna need it."

We both stopped and stared, watching Simona's ponytail bounce behind her as she walked down the street.

"Hey," I said, turning to Pippa. "What was up with that red paint on Simona's hands that day?"

Pippa's mouth dropped open. "You know what? I don't know. Maybe she was throwing red paint at her ex-boyfriend's car or something? Or, maybe, she was the one who did it."

I glanced up at the spot on the window where the paint had been. Even though it had been well scrubbed a dozen times, I could have sworn I still saw a pink sheen to it. "After all, Deena was never one hundred percent sure it was Carl she saw that day."

"I guess we'll never know if we can ever really trust Bakermatic," I said, setting the gift basket down on the floor behind the counter. "But I've got bigger things to worry about now." I leaned against the counter and pondered as Pippa starting piling a tray high with glossy donuts.

"I'm starting to wonder, Pippa, if this should be my new calling."

She glanced up at me, a donut stuck on the end of her tongs. "What, running a bakery?" she asked.

"No!" I said, laughing as I stuck my tongue out at her. "I mean, solving mysteries."

"The Bakery Detectives," Pippa laughed.

I nodded. "The Bakery Detectives."

Thank You!

Thanks for reading *A Pie to Die For*. I hope you enjoyed reading the story as much as I enjoyed writing it. If you did, it would be awesome if you left a review for me on Amazon and/or Goodreads.

If you would like to know about all my new releases and have the opportunity to get free books, make sure you sign up for our Cozy Mystery Newsletter.

FairfieldPublishing.com/cozy-newsletter

On the next page, I have included a preview of my next book, *The Antique Store Murder*. It will be available on Amazon in April, 2016.

I am also including a preview of the first cozy mystery from my friend Miles Lancaster. It starts on the next page. I really hope you like it!

Stacey Alabaster

Preview: The Antique Store Murder

Blood red jam seeped out of the center of the body as I pressed down onto the pastry, causing it to drip out of the center of the donut.

The smell of fresh cinnamon sugar, sprinkled all over the donut hit my nose. *I need to taste test—for the good of the business.* I justified to myself before I popped the soft warm donut in my mouth. "Mmm Mmm Mmm."

I started coughing and Pippa had to thump the back of my chest as the first customers of the day started to pour into my shop, Rachael's Boutique Bakery. I straightened up and put on my brightest smile, my eyes still watering from my near-choke experience. Probably served me right. I looked down at the trays of jam donuts and then at the line of early bird customers. We'd be lucky if we had enough to last the morning rush.

One after another they came, flooding the shop and making my heart leap for joy. Only a few months earlier I had thought my poor little bakery was going to perish. Now it was flourishing more than ever.

Only one little teeny tiny problem: success can lead to complacency. Worse than that: it can lead to boredom.

My fingers were itching, and not just to knead dough, not just to bake and create. I wanted to solve another mystery.

"Oi!" Pippa reached over and gave me a playful shove. "Stop daydreaming about solving mysteries," she scolded. Her hair was bright blue this month and it was often a talking point for customers when they came into the shop. "It's blueberry," she would say with a wink, before trying to sell them one of our fresh blueberry muffins. At least she was creative.

"I'm not," I protested, standing up quickly, embarrassed. "That's all in the past. I'm 100% focused on the bakery now."

Pippa shot me a skeptical look as a lock of bright blue hair fell into her eyes. "Doesn't look that way to me." She took her apron off, the morning rush over, and began to count the money in the cash register, one of her new tasks as assistant manager. "Besides," she said with a cheeky raise of the eyebrow. "You know I've got plenty of real mysteries for you to solve, if you're into paranormal."

I groaned. "I wouldn't call those 'real' mysteries, Pippa. I wish you'd stop hanging out with those people." I couldn't care less about hunting cryptids or chasing ghosts, or whatever it was that Pippa and her new friends were into. I'd had a taste of the real thing—solving a real life murder, and, although I've never wish for harm to fall anyone, I couldn't help missing the rush that had come with being an amateur detective. Belldale had been quiet—and yes, boring—for the past two months.

"Our best morning yet!" Pippa announced with glee, as she pushed the register closed again. "A new record."

We high-fived and I grinned.

Sure, solving mysteries was fun, but it didn't put money in the bank. The bakery did. And I had to remember that.

Besides, a new record day of earnings meant I could finally take the plunge and do something even more exciting than solving a murder mystery.

I took a deep breath and followed Pippa over to an empty table as she took her break. I let her eat anything she liked on a break and today she had chosen a Danish pastry.

"Guess what Pippa?" I sat across from her, too excited to eat anything myself as I readied myself to tell her the exciting news.

I could see her mind already starting to work as she looked up at the ceiling and poked her tongue out of the corner of her mouth.

"Hmm, you're finally going on a date with Detective Whitaker?"

"Pippa! No! Don't be silly."

"Well has he called you yet?"

"Pippa...no...that doesn't matter. That's not my news and I wouldn't be excited if it was. Keep guessing."

She placed her danish down and chewed on it, still pondering.

"You've found another mystery to solve? Is that it? I know that would make you excited."

I shook my head. "That's not it."

She threw her hands up in the air and said she was ready to give up. "Besides, cookies need to come out of the oven," she said, hurrying over to the oven to pull out the tray before she gave one last wild guess. "You've won the lottery?"

"Nope!" I said, pleased that she hadn't guessed. "I'm expanding the bakery. I'm purchasing the antiques shop next door!"

The tray of cookies she was carrying crashed to the ground.

Not exactly the reaction I was hoping for. Was she happy? Excited? Her wide eyes said otherwise.

"Rachael," Pippa whispered as she gripped the collar of my shirt. "You can't purchase the antiques shop!" Her face was as white as a ghost.

"Pippa!" I shook her off me and brushed off my shirt. "Why ever not? I thought you would be pleased for me? For us." Pippa had a....let's just say 'issue' keeping a job longer than a week. Her tenure at my bakery, two months now, was easily the longest she had ever stayed at a job. I thought she would be thrilled to know that she had secure employment in a blossoming business.

"I'm pleased that the bakery is successful." Pippa stopped and glanced over her shoulder in the direction of the antiques shop, as though she could see through the brick wall. She shook her head slowly. "But you can't buy the shop next door." She turned back to face me, her eyes still as wide as pies.

"Rachael, that place is haunted."

I scoffed. "Oh come on Pippa. I know you believe a lot of outlandish things, but this is too much."

"Rachael!" Her voice was high and indignant. "You must have heard the rumors."

I turned back to the counter, in a little bit of a huff now, feeling as though Pippa was raining on my parade. "No, I haven't heard any rumors." I shot Pippa a look. "But I don't really frequent the same places you do."

I was talking about the Belldale Haunted House tour and the Belldale Paranormal Club. Pippa had recently joined said club and had attended several of their tours, which took place after dark and involved dragging locals and tourists alike around Belldale's 'most haunted' homes and buildings. Pippa had come back to our apartment following these tours and given me several breathless accounts of how amazing and eye-opening they were, while I tried to listen with a straight face.

Pippa let out a deep sigh. "The haunted house tour was very informative when it came to the antiques shop."

"Pippa that whole tour is just a scam to get money. It's a bit of entertainment. You can't take the stories seriously. You can't let them impact a business decision."

"But the rumors have been around for way longer than the tour has been running!" Pippa caught the skeptical look on my face and lowered her voice. "You know the painting that's been sitting in the corner for years. The one of the young girl and boy?"

I swallowed. I knew the one she meant. A large watercolor in bronze framing of a pair of children, painted like they were in the 1940s, but cartoon like. Both the children had been painted to have large cartoon like eyes that dwarfed their faces. The eyes seemed to follow you. I always hurried past it because it gave me the creeps. The painting had been in the store, in the same place, in the front window, for as long as I could remember.

"What about it?" I picked up a cloth and began to wipe the tables, as though I wasn't really interested in what Pippa was saying. When actually I had my ears keenly pricked, waiting for her response.

"They say that painting is haunted. That's why it never sells. No one wants it in their homes."

I stood up straight. "Well that's the silliest thing I've ever heard." I shook my head. "That painting doesn't sell because it is overpriced. Not to mention ugly. Besides, the painting won't be there once I buy the store. None of the antiques will."

Pippa shook her head. "The rumors say that the boy and girl who live in the painting…"

"The boy and girl who are painted onto the canvas," I corrected her.

Pippa ignored me. "The story goes, that they live in the shop. They've lived there for decades. That's why the painting never sells. They don't let anyone buy it. They can't be moved from their home. Rachael, if you buy the shop and try to get rid of the painting, then the children will be very upset. They will curse you!"

I was just standing there staring at Pippa like she had lost her mind. "Okay Pippa, that's a great story. But unfortunately, some of us have to live in reality. Some of us have a business to run."

"Rachael, I am warning you. If you buy that shop and try to get rid of the painting, you will pay the price."

***

I told Pippa I needed to run to the post office and do some errands so that she wouldn't try to stop me. As soon as I was out the door, I went in the opposite direction, towards the mortgage firm where I was meeting the landlord of the antiques shop, a tall thin man called Bruce who had a pencil thin moustache and eyebrows that always looked raised.

He pushed the contract over towards me and I gave it a look over. "That should all be in order.

Yes, I decided. *This is the right time to do it. Time to take the plunge.*

"Great," I said, smiling at him. "I'll give it to my lawyer to look over, and then sign it. I should have it back to you by tomorrow."

"Tomorrow?" he asked, a little nervously, his raised eyebrows disappearing even further up into his forehead. "Why can't you sign them now? I can assure you everything is above board."

I stood up as a show of confidence. "I just need to make sure everything is in place. Tomorrow will be fine, won't it? Not much can change by tomorrow!"

As soon as I stepped out of the bank, the heaven's opened on me and I stared up at the sky, mouth agape, to find the sky, which had been a bright blue before I'd stepped into the bank, was now practically black, filled with angry swirling clouds that were spewing icy rain all over the streets.

And I didn't even have an umbrella with me.

Using my purse as a shield over my head, I raced back to the bakery, cursing the fact that I hadn't read the weather report.

"It wasn't predicted in the weather report," Pippa informed me warily as I shook myself off, causing a small puddle to form in the entryway of the shop. "Where have you been?" She stopped frothing the milk for the cappuccino she was making and looked me up and down.

"I told you, the post office."

"The way to the post office is totally covered. You've been the other way."

Sprung.

"Okay, fine," I said with a sigh, as I pulled the contract out of my bag to show to her.

"Oh Rachael." Her face was grave. "Aren't you going to listen to anything I told you?"

"Pippa, it will be fine. I can't be put off by a silly superstation."

She handed the contract back to me and crossed her arms. "It's more than that Rachael." She shivered and looked up at the ceiling. "You've set events in motion now by taking that contract."

"I haven't signed it yet," I pointed out. Not that I believed anything she was going on about.

"That doesn't matter Rachael. It has already starting."

I sighed and took off my soaking wet pea coat and hung it on a hook by the door. As I stepped back towards the counter I heard a snapping sound and heard my heavy coat fall to the floor, the hook taking off a chunk of paint and plaster with it as it tumbled after the coat

"It's just an old hook, Pippa," I said, staring at it. "And the coat was heavy from the rain."

"I'm telling you..."

There was a crashing sound and all of a sudden we were encased in darkness. Outside the sky was so dark that without lights in the shop there was no light at all.

Pippa let out a shriek and rubbed her arms as though she had the worst case of the chills the world had ever seen.

"It's just a broken fuse, Pippa," I said, catching the gleam of the whites of her eyes. I could tell what she was thinking before she even said it. "Or a power line has come down in the storm. Calm down Pippa. Think rationally."

"It's the curse Rachael. It's already started."

Thanks for reading a sample of my first book, *The Antique Store Murder*. I really hope you liked it.

It will be available on Amazon in April, 2016.

Make sure you turn to the next page for the preview of Murder in the Mountains.

Stacey Alabaster

Preview: Murder in the Mountains

Screams were not a normal part of the workday at Aspen Breeze. When Jennifer heard the anguished cry of the maid, she ran around the desk and sprinted out the door. Clint, not through with his breakfast, followed at her heels. The door to the room had been left open. The maid stood on the thick burgundy carpet in front of the unmade bed and pointed at the hot tub.

Water remained in the tub, but it wasn't swirling. The occupant, a red-haired, slightly chubby man whose name Jennifer had forgotten, was face down. His blue running shorts had changed to a darker blue due to dampness. Reddish colorations marred his throat. Another dark spot of blood mixed with hair around his right temple. Pale red splotches marred the water.

For a moment, she felt like the ground had opened and she had fallen into blackness. Legs weakened. Knees buckled. She shook her head and a few incoherent syllables came from her mouth. Clint's arm grasped her around her waist.

"Step back. It's okay," he said.

It was a silly thing to say, he later thought. Clearly, it was not okay, but in times of stress people will often say and do stupid things.

He eased her backward, and then sat her down on the edge of the bed. He walked back and took a second look at the hot tub. He had seen dead bodies when he covered the police beat. It wasn't a routine occurrence, but he had stood in the rain twice and on an asphalt pavement once as EMTs covered a dead man and lifted him into an ambulance.

By the time he turned around, Jennifer was back on her feet and the color had returned to her cheeks.

She patted her maid on the shoulder. "Okay, it's all right. We have to call the police. You can go, Maria. Go to the office and lay down."

"Yes, ma'am."

She glanced at Clint and saw he had his cell phone out.

"...at the Aspen Breeze Lodge," he was saying. "There's a dead body in Unit Nine. It doesn't look like it was a natural death." He nodded then slipped the cell phone in his pocket. "They said the chief was out on a call but should be here within fifteen minutes."

"Good." Jennifer put her hands on her hips. Her gaze stared toward the hot tub. A firm, determined tone came back in her voice.

"Clint, those marks on his throat. The red on his forehead. This wasn't an accident, was it?"

"We can't really say for sure. He might have tripped and hit...." The words withered in the face of her laser stare. "I doubt it. I...I really can't say for sure but...I doubt it."

They looked at one another for a few seconds. Light yellow flames rose up from the artificial fireplace and the crackling of wood sounded from the flames. Jennifer sighed. She realized there was nothing to do except wait for the police.

The silence was interrupted by a tall, thin man, unshaven as yet, who rushed in.

"Bill, what are you doing with the door open? It's still cold...." He stopped as if hit by a stun gun. Eyes widened. He stumbled but caught himself before he fell to the carpeted floor. "Oh, no! What happened?"

Jennifer shifted into her professional tone as manager. "We don't know yet, sir. I assume you knew this man."

He nodded weakly. "Yeah, Bill's been a friend of mine for years."

"I remember you from when you checked in yesterday, but I'm sorry I can't remember your name."

"Dale Ramsey."

Ramsey had a thin, pale face that flashed even paler. There was a chair close to him and he collapsed in it. He had an aquiline nose and chin but curly brown hair. His hand went to his heart.

"Sorry you had to learn about your friend's death this way, Mr. Ramsey," Jennifer said. "I regret to say I've forgotten his name too."

"Bill Hamilton."

Jennifer turned back to Clint. "Do you think we should move the body? Put it on the rug and cover it with a blanket?"

Clint shook his head. "I think the police would prefer it stay right where it is, at least for now."

Jennifer nodded. A steel gaze came in her eyes. She looked at Ramsey, who almost flinched. Then he shook slightly as if dealing with the aftermath of a panic attack.

"Mr. Ramsey, I am the owner of this Lodge and obviously I am very upset someone used it as a place for murder. So I trust you won't mind if I ask you a few questions - just to aid the police, of course."

Ramsey swallowed, or tried to. It looked like a rock had lodged in his throat. "Of course not. I...I do will anything I can to help," he said.

"Six single individuals checked into my lodge last night. That's a little unusual. I was commenting on that to Clint just last night. Now it turns out that you knew the deceased. Do you know the other four people who checked in?"

"Yes...I...yes."

There was a pause and Jennifer noted the look of sadness in his eyes.

"I realize you are upset, Mr. Ramsey, so just relax and take your time."

"We are all members of the Centennial Historical Society. All of us are history buffs," he finally answered.

"Why did you all check in here?"

Ramsey shifted in his chair. "This may sound unbelievable."

"Let's try it and see," Jennifer said.

"About a hundred and twenty-five years ago there was a Wells Fargo gold shipment in these parts. An outlaw gang headed by a man nicknamed The Falcon stole it. He got the name because he liked heights and the Rocky Mountains and had actually trained a falcon at one time. Rumor is, the gang got about a hundred thousand worth in gold, coins and bars. What's known is the gang drifted apart and a few members got shot, but the gold was never found. We believe it's buried very close by, up in the Rocky Mountain National Forest."

Jennifer nodded. The entrance to the forest was less than five miles from Aspen Breeze. All drivers had to do was turn left when they left the lodge and they would hit the entrance in about ten minutes.

"The Rocky Mountain National Forest is a huge area, thousands of miles there of virtually unexplored wilderness. You better have a specific location or you'll spend your lifetime looking and never find anything," she said.

'We have researched this gang for years. We think we know approximately where the gold was buried. It's more than just recovering the gold. This would be a historical find of enormous significance. We were going up there today to try to find the site."

"Maybe someone didn't want to share," Clint said.

Ramsey shook his head. "I doubt it. I've known these people for years. I don't think anyone would kill Bill. Besides, whoever it was would have to kill all of us too if he wanted to keep the gold to himself. Bill was in the high tech field, lower management, but he also liked the wilderness. He knew this forest better than any of us. We were counting on him to help find the site of the gold. He had searched the forest a number of times during the past five years.

I came out with him a few times. He thought he knew where the outlaws had hid their stash. He shared his opinions with us, but he was the one with the most expertise. Eddie, Eddie Tercelli, one of our group, is the second most knowledgeable about the location. He was out a few times too with Bill searching. But it would be tough for him to find the place on his own."

A blue light waved and flickered in the room. They heard a car door open and then slam shut. They looked up as the officer walked in. He wore a fine, crisp blue uniform with a bright silver badge. He had a slight paunch over his belt, but it didn't make him look old or slow. The intense gray eyes under the rim of the black police cap took in everything. His revolver was clearly visible on his right hip.

"Chief Sandish," Clint said, nodding.

Thanks for reading a sample of my first book, *Murder in the Mountains*. I really hope you liked it.

It will be available on Amazon in April, 2016.

Miles Lancaster

Printed in Great Britain
by Amazon

14749883R00093